"In *Leafskin*, Miranda Schmidt's remarkable first novel, short chapters as lyrical as prose poems weave and twine to probe what it means to make something grow in this time of climate destruction: a tree, a marriage, a poem, a painting, a friendship, a child. By developing the fluidity of our most important relationships, those between the human and natural worlds, between reality and myth, and between genders and even in the presence of ice storms, heat domes, and wildfires, it's possible for the characters—and us—to find connection, creativity, and rebirth."

Maya Sonenberg, author of *Bad Mothers, Bad Daughters*

"Miranda Schmidt's novel *Leafskin* and the fictional family that inhabits these pages live in the same world we all occupy at this precise moment, whether it is our own personal story or the stories embedded in every news feed—climate crisis, IVF treatments, and even wildfires. What makes this novel so powerful is the fictional fabric of the narrative that weaves a lyrical and sensory-driven voice that take the reality of today's news and delivers it not from a bully pulpit, but with every prick of a needle, with each breath of smoke, with the embrace of those who love. Below the treetops, the world is called the forest's understory. In *Leafskin*, we find ourselves to be that understory."

Shawn Wong, author of *American Knees*

"Rippling with glimpses of folklore and mystery, *Leafskin* calls our attention to the gravity of extreme weather events—with an admirable lightness and strangeness of touch. Schmidt's protagonist Jo is a sensitive, anxious but determined heroine—and through her eyes we see how much goes into the making of a child. A fresh, intricately-written and dreamlike novel about love, creativity and the natural world."

Jane Borodale, author of *The Book of Fires* and *The Knot*

Leafskin

by Miranda Schmidt

STILL
HOUSE
PRESS

FIRST EDITION

All rights reserved.

No part of this book may be reproduced without written permission from the publisher.

All inquiries may be directed to

Stillhouse Press
4400 University Drive, 3E4
Fairfax, VA 22030
www.stillhousepress.org

Stillhouse Press is an independent, student- and alumni-run nonprofit press based out of Northern Virginia and operated in collaboration with Watershed Lit: Center for Literary Engagement and Publishing Practice at George Mason University.

LCCN: 2024945028

ISBN-13: 978-1-945233-28-9

EPUB ISBN: 978-1-945233-29-6

Cover Art: Alejandra Giron
Jacket Design: Michael McDermott
Interior Design: Paul Logan IV

for Ash and Elanor

and for the sequoias

who watch over this place

Part One

Alight

1

Everywhere, the smoke. Gray and heavy. Sharp in the lungs. When Jo takes out the trash that evening, it engulfs her. She returns to the house sputtering—eyes burning, nose dripping—as if she's come close to uncanny dry drowning.

Inside, she stares out the window. The backyard sequoia stands guard in the gray. The neighbor's cat slinks across the roots, miserably making his rounds. That morning, Jo put out a dish of water for the usual animals in case they got thirsty in the smudged acrid heat, in case they couldn't find clean water in all this ash. But no one came. All day, she hasn't seen one squirrel. Not one glimpse of the wings of a crow.

Behind the tree's branches, the sun is a winnowed spot of fogged redorange blazing. It hangs in the haze of the sky, threatening flame. Soon, it will set, and night will come, and Jo will lay in bed, feeling the heaviness in her lungs, the way it sinks her down into a place in her mind she prefers not to go—a parched scratchy place. Small as cramped handwriting. Blank as new paper. In that place, she can sense the death coming—the warping of seasons and ecosystems, the cracking of icebergs, the mass extinction of species, the loss of the bees. It is the place where forests die, drained by drought, engulfed in fire, drowned.

"It's that time of night," Liam says behind her, pulling her attention from the window.

"Right," Jo says. "Be right there."

This isn't supposed to be happening. It isn't supposed to be the third day the metro area is blanketed in smoke. Fires don't act like this here. This is her tree-filled city—home to oak, maple, fir, home to steady rain and fern green. This gray shouldn't come from smoke, but from clouds and mist and drizzle.

"They're evacuating south of the highway," Liam tells her when she joins him in the bathroom.

He's gotten it all ready while he's been waiting for her: the alcohol wipe, the syringe, the bandage laid out on the edge of the sink. So familiar, now, the routine.

"That's not possible," she says.

"Shouldn't be. But here we are."

She lowers the waist of her jeans and holds it, leaning forward, while Liam positions himself behind her, slides the needle in, pushes down, pulls out, practiced now: quick but still painful. The progesterone shots are worse by far than the battalion they ringed round her belly button for IVF. These shots ache where the others merely pinched—sharp and just skin deep. These are deep tissue shots with their big needles and viscous liquid. They are serious now, preparing her womb for an embryo. Progesterone is the hormone that will keep the potential baby in, that will soften her structures, loosen the muscles and ligaments so the baby can eventually fit through the birth canal. She can feel, already, the way the hormone is liquefying her. It sinks her, fogging her mind like breath on a winter windowpane.

Liam places the little bandage gently. He is always gentle. He gives her all the shots. That was the agreement they made before they started IVF. She'd take the shots, take the pills, grow the eggs, get the blood draws, do the procedures, and grow—hopefully—the embryo that would be the fetus that would be the baby. But he'd give her the shots. And he'd take her to the appointments so she wouldn't have to be alone in those waiting rooms with all those eager expectant parents-to-be, with all their longing and all their hope and all their despair. Over these weeks, the shots have grown strangely intimate—not sexual, but intimate. At first, they were shaky and fearful. Liam watched the instructional videos while he did them, then checked and double-checked that everything was right. And Jo cringed, held her breath, afraid of the pain or of something going wrong or, worst of all, of the potential for failure. But now, she appreciates how her husband is so careful as he chooses the spot, the gentle firmness in his hands as he pushes the needle in, then pulls it out and holds the clean gauze over the puncture, the encouraging smile he gives her after. Each time, it reminds her why she loves him.

"Should we be…doing something?" Jo asks, pulling her jeans back up and glancing out the window as the sky darkens into night.

She isn't sure what she means. She doesn't know what she imagines they could do. She's been staring at her phone all day. The maps show a whole region is on fire. Between the ocean and the mountains: a giant wall of tiny, animated flames. Color-coded evacuation zones with pop-ups about emergency shelters. Color-coded air quality reports. That morning, they'd watched the AQI map turn purple; the air moved so far into hazardous it could no longer be contained in red. The danger is everywhere. There is nowhere to go and nothing to be done. But this apocalyptic feeling, the simmering anger of the hazy sun, the deathly silence that engulfs them, seems to demand some kind of action.

Liam shakes his head. "They're saying stay inside. Keep things shut up. Wait it out, I guess. In the city, we're safe from the fires, at least. I just wish we had air purifiers. It's so stupid not to. I'm so stupid not to have thought of that before. Now everywhere is sold out."

The sharp edges of his worry frighten her, and she thinks of the embryos—frozen and waiting for just the right time in her cycle, for the moment when the pills and the shots have done their work to make her ready. Will the clinic be open? Will they make the appointment? Or will they have to wait yet another month to do it? It is this waiting, she thinks, that has been hardest. The month to recover from the IVF. The almost, now, another month to recalibrate her cycle. And always, in the back of her mind, those embryos, made from possibilities they pulled from her body and his, those uncanny seeds of potential caught in a moment of time she is moving further from every day.

2

She does not sleep that night. She sits at her desk and scribbles incoherently, attempting a poem and failing, once again, to find it. She thinks of the sequoia outside, branches extending over the house, trunk enveloped in nightmare gray. She can't find the words for it, can't find the words for anything. She'd like to blame the smoke or the hormones, but it's more than that, farther back, entrenched somewhere, buried beneath this stable life she and Liam have been making.

"You have to choose," Ness told her once. They were sitting at their spot by the river, beneath the willows. Jo had her notebook. Ness had her sketchpad. She remembers the way Ness would look at the water, the intensity of focus as she captured the shapes the current made.

"Art or normal life," Ness said. "You can't have both. The two don't hold together."

She tries not to think of Ness's postcard sitting in the drawer of her desk. It arrived days ago, before the smoke, before the air became hazardous, back when the mail was still coming. She'd picked it up and known, immediately, who it was from. Who but Ness would send a card covered in swirling paint? She'd known, also, that she could not read it. Not yet. She'd put it in the drawer and tried to forget. But it still tugs at her. So close.

And outside, the sequoia, roots spanning just underground, close to the surface and wide, holding everything.

3

Jo and Liam had first seen the house that would become theirs on a Saturday early that spring. They drove down the tree-lined city street and thought the neighborhood felt pleasant, like a place you could have a home in. There was still snow on the ground when they pulled the car up and spotted their real estate agent across the road. By then, the open houses had become a weekend routine. It always made Jo sad, the houses up for sale, the staged rooms, the crowds of hungry buyers assessing the attributes of a home as if it were a mere appliance.

That morning, they walked up the driveway and into the house and found ten more people in the living room. The house was unassuming from the outside, a single-story ranch that didn't stand out from its neighbors bumping up on either side, but inside, it had what their real estate agent called "that extra something." She pointed out the hard-wood floors, the custom countertops, the way it all came together into a kind of coziness that was hard to describe. It was a nice house, a welcoming house, but there was a tidy domesticity to it that frightened Jo. She caught the soft scent of baby powder in the air, and she knew this was a house for having children in. The knowledge made the house suddenly small and cramped with expectation. So, when they pushed through the crowd in the master bedroom and opened the doors to the backyard, the step outside into the chill spring air was relief.

That's when Jo met the sequoia.

Seeing the sequoia too, Liam was muttering with the agent, "Do you think there's going to be a big bidding war for this one?"

"In this market," the agent said, "there's always a bidding war. But it's a small house. Asking's low. It probably won't go above your range."

Jo was already walking toward the tree, standing beneath them, looking up into their branches that rose forever. The cover of fallen needles crunched beneath her feet, the scent of evergreen. She gazed at the tree's bark, wondered at the way it furled down and encircled the trunk that was so much larger than she could wrap her arms around. She could feel the tree's roots spread beneath her. She knew very little about sequoias then. But she understood their root systems were both expansive and strangely shallow for such large trees.

She didn't touch the trunk. Not yet. She didn't run her fingers over that bark to brush the rough ripples. The yard was crowded, and she didn't want to seem too odd. Instead, she looked up. High in those branches, a crow perched, looking down at her. The bird didn't make a sound, just that

looking, a whole dark-eyed world

taking her measure.

"We should probably go see the next one before the open house ends," Liam said, coming up beside her. The warmth of his hand reminded her of her own. She felt the shape of her palm against his, beckoning her back to herself.

Jo nodded, still partly caught in the tree's branches, roots, bark, crow, the way they all watched her.

Walking back to the car, Liam was chatty—excited, she could tell, but trying not to be.

"It's a nice house. And so much room for gardens," he was saying. "We probably won't get it, though. All those people. There are going to be so many offers."

Jo looked back at the house, at the sequoia rising up behind it, and had that feeling of knowing she sometimes got around trees, a kind of extra sense, like hearing a voice without hearing anything. They would get the house. They would think it was because they offered high, wrote a nice letter to the owners, had a good real estate agent. But those were just particulars. It wasn't up to them. This was the sequoia's domain. And, for whatever mysterious reason, the tree had chosen them.

4

Now, morning. Liam making coffee. When she comes into the kitchen, he hands her a mug and tries one of his reassuring smiles.

"We aren't supposed to use the stove except for boiling water," he tells her. "They say not to make any more smoke."

She nods.

His face looks drawn and worried. The shadows under his eyes tell her he hasn't slept well either. He sits at the kitchen table, sipping his coffee while he types on his laptop. Outside the window, the haze of the air.

"How are you feeling?" she asks, sitting across from him.

He shakes his head. "I've been trying to put together an email for members. Tell them what to do for the plants. Figure out what this means for care and harvesting."

Jo is scrolling through alerts on her phone, then putting it down, then picking it back up again. Liam keeps typing. As the program manager of one of the city's community garden nonprofits, he is needed now. Jo tries to imagine it, having something to do in response to all this. The relief of action, the responsibility.

"I have to go water our plants," Liam says, setting his mug down.

"Don't stay out in the smoke too long."

"I won't," Liam promises.

The screen of her phone is filled with images of fire, smoke, families fleeing to evacuation shelters, parking lots filled with cars packed with whatever could be taken from their homes before they burned.

"Remember, we can't eat anything straight from the garden for a while. It's all covered in ash. We have to wash it well."

Jo nods.

She is staring at the screen of maps again. Each fire bleeding into the next. Uncanny walls of flame. A whole region set alight.

"What if this is normal now?" Liam asks, wrapping a scarf around his face. His eyes look haunted by a future he cannot imagine. She knows he does not want an answer. She lets the question hang in the air between them.

When he is outside, she watches him through the window, the way he reaches out to hold the graying leaves of the tomatoes as if he is comforting small distraught children, fathering the end of the world.

5

She sits down at her desk and tries to work. Her laptop dings at her, messages coming through from colleagues stuck at home. A forwarded article about the fires. A company-wide email about the office being closed. A joke about how snow days will be ash days now. A reminder of a deadline for the web copy she hasn't been able to bring herself to touch yet. She opens the window with her notes, pulls the creative brief up beside it, tries to come up with a headline.

The client, maker of sustainable paper cups, likes words that are friendly. Things that don't imply guilt or judgement. They want their copy chipper and accessible. And she wonders if this is what they will all be doing, what she will be doing, when the world ends: pretending it isn't while trying to sell more disposable dishware.

She shuts the laptop. She opens the drawer of her desk. The postcard stares up at her. She reaches for it.

It's an unusual card, hand-painted. She can feel the texture of the brush strokes with her fingertips as she holds the card between them, that familiar prickling sensation of waking.

Ness's paintings always held a kind of undertow, an almost magnetized quality to pull the gazer inward more quickly and more thoroughly than expected. Jo is not prepared to find it here too, even in the small postcard size. Ness has painted a coastline, a forest and an oceanscape where two ecosystems meet.

"Ecotones," Jo remembers Ness saying back in college when they had such conversations, "are liminal spaces. Generative spaces. New things are born there. Old ways die."

In the tiny postcard painting, the wind whirls the trees and the waves. Jo traces the movement with her fingertips, trying to follow the brushstrokes. Ness's brush. Held in Ness's hand. Familiar. The brushstrokes grip her like they always used to, getting inside her, changing her rhythms. Jo feels, for a moment, the touch of hands through them, across the distances of time and space. Once, they swept over her body, curling around her breasts, over her stomach. Now, they sweep through this landscape. Ness has made it just for her, Jo realizes. A meeting of sorts. Looking into it, Jo feels outside herself. Her self is not hers anymore.

Jo can almost see Ness's eyes watch through the colors. The way the atmosphere would change around her when she walked into a room. The way she could make it all circle her, as if she held the very center of gravity inside her.

Jo turns the postcard over.

Ness's writing fills the card, runs up and around its edges, seeking more space. It's hard to read, the familiar/unfamiliar of it. Jo hasn't seen her writing in years. But here it is. Words. And so many of them. Her eyes adjust, find the meaning.

Ness is coming back. She'll be here in a couple weeks. For an art show at their old university. Will Jo come? They could watch the eclipse together. She'd love to see her again. She'd love to catch up.

Her name signed at the bottom. And a phone number.

Jo has never, in all the years since Ness left her, had her phone number. Only when they dated in college, only then, and then, Ness was always ignoring her phone. Never picked up. Never returned calls. Was always too caught up in her art for such mundane concerns.

In the years since, Ness has written to her a handful of times. But the return addresses have never worked. By the time Jo's letters reach them, Ness has moved on and the letters come back unopened. Ness never leaves a forwarding address. She's never given an email or a number. Until now.

Still, Jo is wary. Ness has said this before, about seeing her again, about catching up. She's written the words and then vanished again for years at a time.

Jo looks at the number, wonders at the power she feels holding that handful of digits. She could call. She could call right now if she wanted to. The thought terrifies her. She drops the card on her desk.

6

When they got the house, Liam couldn't believe their luck, but Jo wasn't surprised. A few weeks later, they were packing their things into the moving van to drive across town.

"Our first house," he kept saying.

They'd been saving for years. And now, here they were: homeowners.

"Well, we did it before forty," Liam said, laughing at their good fortune. "Just under the wire."

They didn't say it then, but she knew they both thought it, that maybe, now they had a house, the child would come. They'd been trying for years, but no luck. Now, they were trying not to think too much about it, the growing suspicion that something was wrong, the fear that she would soon be too old, that she could be already. And because they were trying not to think about it, because she didn't want to worry him too soon or give him a false sense of hope, she didn't tell him, then, that her period was late by a week, that she was hopeful.

So, he didn't know, a few days later, when she'd taken her lunch break to go clean out the last things in the apartment, about her hope. And she couldn't tell him, when, alone in their empty former home, thinking about how small it seemed without their furniture to shape the rigid square box of it, she felt the familiar cramping, found the familiar spots of blood. She searched under the sink, pulled out the stray bag of menstrual pads she'd left there and forgotten about when she'd switched to the cup. She was relieved she hadn't told him. It was a silly hope. She was relieved he wasn't with her to hide the disappointment from.

She thought she'd always known she'd be a mother. It was never a question of if, just when. And she knew the kind of mom that she would be, how she'd introduce her child to the world, all the wonders of it: the way the summer light glowed through the maple leaves, how the air smelled damp and loamy in the fall, the slugs that lingered under rocks, the ripe of wild strawberries. She'd wondered, too, at what the feeling of growing a child would be. Would it be like a seed sprouting, or would it be like a fern that unfurls? Would she feel the magic of creation in it, or would she just feel taken over? It frightened her, how much of herself she knew she would give.

In the empty apartment, because Liam wasn't there, she let herself cry while she swept, alone, missing, already, the tiny, cramped space of it, the years they'd spent in it, the life they'd made there. She wept with the sadness of leaving and with the fear of what they were leaving for. What if, she wondered, they couldn't have a child? What then?

She didn't like to think of how much of their marriage was built on child-wanting. Back at the end of college, on their third date, he'd let it slip. "Someday, I really want to have kids." And she'd seen it, right then, the family they could have, the life they could make together. She'd wanted it with so much of herself, it terrified her. She'd felt the wanting all through her body, deep inside, a vast yawning hunger that only grew when she noticed it.

"Not now, of course," he'd said, and, even then, she could see his worry that he'd made a mistake, gone too far too soon and scared her. "You know, eventually."

She'd nodded. "Yes," she'd told him. "Eventually."

Eventually was now. And now, she was bleeding.

That evening, after they'd turned in the key to their apartment, picked up a bottle of wine from the grocery store, and driven across town to their new house, where, amidst all the unpacked boxes, they opened it, pouring it into mugs like they had when they were younger, before they owned things like wine glasses, she told him she wanted to set up an appointment at a fertility clinic.

"It's time," she said. "It's now or never, I think."

Liam nodded and took her hand in his and kissed her. They lingered in that familiar space where their breaths touched and bore them up, together. In that place, lips close, eyes meeting, Jo always felt like anything was possible, like they could create whole worlds together if they chose.

"I've been thinking that for a while," he admitted. "But I didn't want to rush it. I didn't want to push you."

She sipped the wine. Red. Even with all their things here, she could still smell that baby powder scent. She tried to think of it as a kind of blessing. This house had held children. This house would hold children again. But it still unsettled her, the soft bright smell of it.

7

At night, Jo cannot sleep. Her chest aches. Her breath is heavy inside her. She feels the death in each inhalation, her mind burning gray.

There should be a moon, but Jo cannot find one in the smoke-smudged dark. She imagines the moon hiding, full and silverwhite, behind it all, beyond it. She imagines the moon peering down at them, disappointed.

Jo takes the postcard and her phone to the living room. She dials the number before she has a chance to reconsider. She almost hangs up at the dial tone, the way it breaks into the quiet, its startling reality. But then, the voice, Ness's voice, saying, "Hello?" Not sleepy at all. Clear and awake.

She takes a breath, releases it with a tentative, "Hi."

"Jo?"

Jo nods, remembers the phone, and says, "Yep."

"Jo," Ness says, and she can hear the smile in her voice, can see the way it curves her lips up, that little bit of mischief there. "I knew you'd call."

Jo laughs, off-balance, not wanting to have been so predictable. Of course she called. Of course Ness knew she would.

But she doesn't know what to say now that she has called, now that she has Ness's voice in her ear.

"Did I wake you?" Jo asks, though she knows that she hasn't. She knows what Ness sounds like when waking. The sound

17

of dreams gathered round, fraying but clinging, making her distant.

"No," Ness says. "It's the middle of the night there, isn't it?"

"Yeah."

"I miss those nights. The moonglow through the clouds."

"No moon here tonight."

"Right. You're all smoke and fire out there now, aren't you?"

"Something like that," Jo says, trying to sound neutral, trying not to sound scared or sad. But Ness can hear through it.

"You okay?" she asks, her voice gentle now, concerned.

"We'll be fine," Jo says. "They're predicting rain soon."

"That's good," Ness says, then asks, "What are you up to these days?"

Jo's mind blanks at the question. She can think of nothing interesting to say. Not for Ness. She feels the gap of time, the distance between them, how little they know of each other now.

"We're trying to have a kid," she hears herself tell her.

She doesn't know why she says it. She doesn't know why she thinks Ness will care. Perhaps she says it to prove something, but she isn't sure what or how. In her mind, the memory of that time back in college when they saw a mom in the park trying to coax her toddler back into the car. Jo saying, "When I have kids, we'll stay out in the park all day." Ness scoffing. "I'm never having kids. Real artists don't have that kind of family." And that sharp pain Jo felt, as if Ness had drawn a circle around herself and found Jo wanting, left her out of it.

"Wow," Ness says now, and Jo can't read her voice.

"Yeah."

"You were always going to be a mom."

"Really?"

"Oh definitely. You've got that maternal quality."

"What do you mean?"

"Caring. Stable. Self-sacrificing. Classic mom."

"I'm not *that* maternal," Jo says.

Ness laughs.

"The kid will be lucky to have you."

"Your postcard said you were coming through?" Jo asks, changing the subject.

"I will be. Soon."

"Where are you now?"

"Oh, you know, here and there."

The words falter again. Jo can hear Ness breathing down the line.

"Do you remember that painting I did of you? The one I left?"

"The tree?" Jo asks, though she doesn't need to ask. She knows exactly what painting Ness means.

"You still have it, right?"

There is a hint of anxiety, Jo thinks, in Ness's voice. The small fear that maybe she doesn't have it, that maybe she didn't keep it, that maybe she gave it away or threw it away or destroyed it in her anger at the leaving.

"Of course, I still have it," Jo says. She wants to be the kind of person who would tease the suspense out a little longer, who would make Ness wait and worry. But she doesn't have the heart for it. She doesn't want her to think, not for a moment longer, that her work isn't safe and whole.

Ness's relief is audible when she says, "Oh good. I always liked that painting. I think it might be one of my best."

Jo is surprised by that. She'd thought the painting was only one of many in Ness's shapeshifting women phase. Just another one of her girls turning into something else: a little mythic, a little feminist, a little eerie. Nothing special. Nothing, Jo always thought, compared to what Ness would have been doing later.

"Can I borrow it?" Ness is asking. "For the show? They want something I did in college alongside the new work. You know, encourage the students. You're coming, right? We can watch the eclipse. We'll be able to see totality from there."

And suddenly, it is all too much: the phone call, her voice, the smoke, the memories crowding out the present, the present muddling up the memories. And now, the painting asserting itself again. She can feel the draw of it where it lies, rolled up on the shelf in the hall closet, put away, out of sight. Still, she can see it. She has it memorized. Every color. Every shade and shadow. Every brushstroke. The way it holds her face that is not her face and turns it. The leaves unfurling out of it. The bark encircling, clinging tight, constricting. The terrible weight of the wood.

"Yes," she hears herself saying, agreeing to all of it.

8

Just before dawn, the haze of heavy solitude. Outside the window, nothing stirs. No wind. No birds. Deathly silence. Sequoia in the dark, always and forever in the one same place. Pulled like water to their center. Against the trunk, leaning, eyes closed. Then—

Flash of fire in the choke of smoke. Moving fast on high winds. Dry heat of burning roots. Connections severing faster than the signals sent in warning. Scurries of animals. Nowhere to flee. Feeling of small, desperate feet over trunk, branches, roots. Digging down, climbing up, attempting escape. But no help for them.

    saplings burn first
       generation lost grief
   flames in the dark
       currents the underground

When Jo comes back to herself, she is standing outside, barefoot, toes turned gray with ash. She only half remembers walking from her bed out to the yard. She is under the sequoia. Her hand on their bark feels hot. When she pulls it away, her hand goes suddenly cold. Her whole body shivers, feeling altered in some strange undefinable way. A sensation of hollowing. She thinks of trees burnt by fire, struck by lightning or insects or rot, almost felled, charred but still growing, an impossible space at their center. She can feel the sequoia breathing.

She pulls her sweater around her, runs inside.

9

It was during IVF that she started to make what Liam called her "Wall of Destruction." She'd been collecting the clippings for some time: articles about dying habitats, maps of flooded coastlines, pictures of rapidly vanishing species. She'd kept them in box at first. But, in those weeks of endless shots and doctor visits and blood draws, she found herself pulling them out, tacking them up above her desk. One by one. Soon, the whole wall was filled.

Liam grew concerned.

"Are you sure," he asked, "that you want to be looking at all that all the time?"

"I want to see the shape of it," she told him.

He didn't understand and she couldn't explain it any better. She knew it was odd, this compulsion. As her ovaries filled up with eggs, the drugs making them grow more and more than they ever would without them, she filled up the wall with the facts of devastation. Days dragged on, and her belly bloated. Eggs blossomed in, crowding the rest of her, making her heavy and laden. She tacked up image over image, layering statistics and stories. In the end, she ran out of thumbtacks. In the end, she started piling the papers on her desk, chair, bookshelf, every available space, everything crowded out by the pulped bodies of trees printed with the incremental deaths of the world.

Late that spring, their first in the house, Liam began planting gardens. She'd find him in the mornings with his notebook and coffee, drawing charts of planter beds and labeling them in his tidy handwriting. He bought the starts from the garden store, a compromise with the growing season that had already begun.

"Next year, I'll grow them from seed," he told her.

She watched him plant the tendrils of green in the ground, patting dirt around them, murmuring words of encouragement. She helped as best she could. In between tests and blood draws at the fertility clinic, she watered the sprouts, checked their leaves for hungry insects, listened to Liam as he described how he hoped they would grow: full and strong and thriving.

They did the egg retrieval as the summer began. At the clinic. Liam in the waiting room, nervous. Ready for when they would call him back to the private room to fill the cup with sperm to inject into the eggs. He'd told her on the drive how terrified he was that, after all the shots and blood draws, after everything she'd done, he'd fail the easy part.

She'd laughed. She tried to stop, especially when he looked at her with such hurt and dismay. But she couldn't. She felt the laugh move through her at an unfamiliar frequency—breathy, panicked.

At the clinic, once they had her in the hospital gown, attached to the IV and lying on the bed, the anesthesiologist explained that they would not put her fully out. Just an in-between space. She'd feel sleepy, perhaps confused, but she'd remember.

The sharp of the needle pricking, deep and organ strange. So far inside, it was no longer a part of her body. Her body

turning into something else, a thing not her, wildness ensor-
celled, laid out on this medical bed. And suddenly, she was
a tree.
arm-branches, toe-roots, insides
          layered wood, overburdened
                    fruit to pluck
                              out of her, egg by
                                   egg, seeding

Afterward, they gave her the numbers. A good harvest. She
knew she was supposed to feel happy.

10

Five years ago. Summer. The first time they tried for a child.

Jo and Liam were driving north, returning home from visiting friends. They'd been driving for hours. They had hours more to go. They were driving through the drought of a historically dry season. For miles, there was nothing but brown grass and the shriveled leaves of shrubby oaks. Then they came to the orchards. The trees had been abandoned when the water ran out. Rows and rows of them. Small dead fruit trees, their sun-bleached bonelimbs casting leafless shadows over the cracked dirt. Like ghosts, Jo thought as she watched them through the window, those shadows, those trees that were planted and then left to die, monuments to agricultural betrayal.

"It's criminal," Liam said, glancing out the window as he drove. She could hear the pain in his voice as he looked out at the abandoned orchards. It was the very particular pain that she always noticed in Liam when he witnessed a lack of human care, the pain of a man who had dedicated his life to growing and tending. Humans. Plants. Communities. He did not like to see these things abandoned.

Jo nodded. There was a horror of nothingness when she realized there was no living tree in sight.

Even after they'd passed through those rainless miles, even when they were back amidst the lush leaves and evergreens of her northern forests, Jo could still see those dead trees, could still feel their memory of thirst.

Jo was thinking of dead trees when they decided to break up the drive home and camp.

"We can see the sequoia groves," Liam said, and Jo agreed. She knew sequoias as city trees, growing singularly in parks and yards, giants intentionally planted for effect. She didn't know them in their natural habitats, growing together, old in those rare groves.

Liam turned the car into the nearly empty campground parking lot. Stepping out, Jo stretched stiff legs and breathed the deep scent of sun on evergreen, coming back into her body.

As they unpacked their tent and supplies, walking them down the narrow path to the campsite, Jo sensed the old trees in their lofty stillness, watching. There was, of course, the expected mystery of stateliness. But alongside that, something else, an unexpected warmth that lived between the furry redbrown bark and the boughs that feathered upward, buoyant. All across the ground, the dropped cones were winking up at them with uncanny eyes.

Liam set up the tent. It was her husband who knew how to do these things. Jo was embarrassed never to have learned. She had never camped as a child. Even after all these trips with Liam, she couldn't light a good fire. The lack of skill left her in a very human kind of helplessness. But beneath that, there was something else, something impractical and strange, a wild thrill at what she might discover in the woods without a human light.

"Looks like we're the only ones here," Liam said, looking around at the other campsite, bare of people and their remnants. "There weren't many other cars in the lot."

"Maybe some day trippers," Jo said, wondering whether they should stay the night in a campground with no other people.

Liam grinned. "We might have the place to ourselves."

Alone with the trees, their own sounds seemed loud and intrusive. Jo listened to the dull thuds as Liam drove their plastic tent spikes into the ground. She wanted to tell him to be quieter. She couldn't shake the sense of being watched. By the trees. By other things. She wasn't sure if all that watching was welcoming.

Jo and Liam followed the hiking trail up from the campground and deeper into the forest. They ran into a family heading down to the parking lot to drive back home.

"Pretty empty today," the dad told them as they passed. "We come hiking here most weekends. It's worth the drive. Nice to skip the crowds."

He carried a squirming toddler in the pack on his back. The other child was walking behind, tickling the toddler's legs with a blade of grass as they both giggled. The mom laughed and shook her head.

They didn't see anyone else.

At the top of a hill, they left the path to pick their ways over rocks and look out at the view. The trees spread before them beneath the bright sun.

"Beautiful," Liam said, breathing the clear, warm air.

Jo remembered the orchards from their drive. She could not help but wonder if these woods would still be this green ten summers from now, twenty. How long could the sequoias stand in this place as the climate shifted? She'd read all the informational signs on the way up, all the details of the increasing stress of drought and fire on sequoias. The way their crowns were browning in the summer. How the intensity of the wildfires was beginning to fell even these trees that had been made for them. Their cones opened in dry heat. Their seeds grew in ash. Their bark was made to withstand flame. But not the flames to come.

She didn't say any of it aloud as Liam enjoyed the view. Instead, she took his hand, and he pulled her closer, wrapping his arms around her. His embrace steadied her. It almost convinced her that the world had some solidity. She had the desire, sometimes, to dissolve into him as if she were a raindrop landing on the earth, letting herself take the shape the ground made for her.

In the emptied evening air, off the path, alone and hidden amidst the trees and ferns, they slipped out of their clothes. Liam laid his t-shirt on the ground for them, and, in his arms, Jo allowed herself to feel the true height of their perch, the forest expanding below, the breeze moving over her bare skin, the sky so close, its blue just beginning to deepen as the sun dipped. The wind carried the scent of fading light.

When Liam pulled the condom from the pocket of his jeans, Jo stopped him. He gave her a questioning look.

"What if we started trying?" Jo asked.

"You want to?"

"I think so. If you do."

That night, beneath the tall sequoias, they lit their fire and watched the woods go dark. They talked about how they would bring their future children to this place, how they would teach them to be in the woods early on so it would never be strange to them, so that the forest would always be theirs.

"We'll teach them how to start a fire and how to set up a tent and how to cook outdoors," Liam said, sounding already proud of the future offspring.

"We'll teach them the names of the trees and plants," Jo said, "And how to identify mushrooms."

They laughed at their planning. It all felt so close and so possible.

And Jo was sure then. She could feel it already. The child they were making. The way the creature was finding its way into being inside her, burrowing down in her soil, the tiniest of seeds. A baby born of sky and ground and roots. Around her, the forest watched, so quiet and still and old. A comfort but also something sharper, rougher. The strangeness of the eyes of trees.

After they put out their fire and crawled into the tent, after Liam was sleeping beside her, quiet in the dark that had fallen so completely she was sure if she reached out to touch it, it would drape over her hands, soft and thick like velvet, she heard the noise. A breathing beside her ear. She convinced herself she was only imagining. She reached for Liam, but she could not find him next to her. She tried to speak, but her voice had crept away to hide itself somewhere inside her. Then she heard it again. It grew louder, bolder, and she could not tell where the breath was from. It was beside her and around her. It was inside the tent and outside it. It was an animal. It was a monster. It was a ghost. She listened for Liam next to her, sure that he must hear it too and wake. He didn't move. The breath was all she could hear now, and in the breath, almost, the sound of something that seemed word-like. But no words she could understand.

Fear shifted then, became another shape. And she grabbed for her metal water bottle. She hit it on the tent. At first, just a thwack on the canvas, soft and hissing. Then she found the corner pole that held the tent in place. The clang of metal on metal woke Liam as she hit the pole again and again, harder and louder.

The sound of breathing stopped.

Liam reached for her. She let him take the water bottle from her hands.

"There was something outside," she said. "Trying to get in."

Liam pulled her down beside him and put his arm around her.

"We're safe in here," he said. "Nothing will come in."

He was sleeping again in a moment.

Later, in the middle of the night, when she finally found her way into sleep, the dream. The baby scratching its way up from the underground, through the soil and leaves, moving earth with strong determined limbs, a tiny bulb awakened, muddy with hunger.

In the morning, she woke to a feeling of floating. All around her, the trees and the air, a murmur of leaflungs. As the sun rose, she almost forgot the fears of the night, the clang of the metal, the uneasy dream. Beneath the floor of their tent, she could almost feel the way the roots burrowed groundward, reaching out to hold the whole of the forest.

That summer, for weeks, she dreamed of the baby. A rooting bulby thing. It looked at her with uncanny eyes, all woods and undergrowth. She would wake with a hand on her belly, sensing the certainty of growth.

When she walked to work, it was as if she carried a secret that the whole of the nonhuman world somehow knew too. She passed by a flock of chickadees and their chirps sounded oracular. She saw a raccoon out in the middle of the day and the creature stared back at her like they could see something hidden inside her. A crow followed her, gliding from wire to wire, for three full blocks, when she left the office for lunch. The caws unsettled her with their wild pitch, a beckoning, a recognition.

So, Jo was surprised when, a week late, her period came and the something she thought she could feel became nothing at all.

Later, a year into their trying, Jo told Liam she'd scared away their baby.

"What do you mean?" he asked.

"That first time. In the sequoia grove. When we were camping. I heard a noise, and I banged the metal, and I scared them."

Liam frowned at her. "You can't scare an embryo away like that."

Jo found it difficult to put any of it into words. The way the forest was planting something inside her that night. The wild of it. How she had panicked.

"It was a forest creature," she told him. "The baby. It came from the trees."

"There wasn't a baby," Liam reminded her, an edge of fear creeping into the steady of his voice.

"But there was. I could feel it."

"That's not how it works, Jo. You had a late period, right? It was the first time we tried."

"It was a miscarriage," Jo told him. "I scared the baby away. I didn't understand it. And it left."

A look Jo couldn't read moved over Liam's face. He took a long breath, in and out, and the look left him. He spoke slowly, evenly, rationally.

"Even if it was a miscarriage, that would have meant the embryo simply wasn't viable. You can't frighten away a pregnancy."

"But I did."

She could see the way his eyes were lost, searching through the illogic of her, trying to find the way to lead them both out. She wanted to tell him he couldn't. Instead, she dug in, insisting. "I know I did."

Liam shook his head. "That's not possible."

"But it's true."

She watched him think. She could see the way his mind was tracing backward, seeking the path that had led them here, trying to understand what it was she was saying.

Finally, he put his arm around her.

"I get it. I think. You're feeling guilty. I know your mind works differently than mine. You're creative. You're a poet. You work in metaphor. That's what this is, right? You're telling me you're scared to get pregnant. That there's something uncontrolled about it, something wild, that frightens you. You're saying it sideways, but that's what you mean, right?"

She could tell he expected her to say yes, to look relieved that he knew her mind so well. But she couldn't lie to him.

"No," she said. "It's not."

She couldn't hide her disappointment, but she tried. They didn't talk about it again after that. But she couldn't shake the growing knowledge that they lived in two separate worlds, running parallel.

11

She is back in their bedroom, now, awake and watchful as the sun rises in its apocalyptic colors, hardly changing the gray hue of the world.

It isn't as if she hasn't thought about it. She thinks about it all the time. She knows raising a child in a time of climate change will be hard. But she always thought that the difficulty would be different. That it would be more subtle than this. That it would be about the unease of dry summers, the slow disappearance of insects, the knowledge of encroachment, boundaries blurring in an expansion of ocean and desert. But she thought, somehow, that she could keep the child safe in it, teach them to love a world and mourn it and try to save it all at once. How to feel all of these things without freezing in the fear of it. They'd sit beneath the sequoia, and she would teach the child the names of plants, the myths of animals. And the child would dig in the roots, feel the rough bark, know the scent of fallen needles and cones in the sun. And she'd tell them how sequoia cones open with fire, how the seeds are freed in heat. And they would see in their mind a glow unfurling in the blaze that burns whole forests while creating the perfect conditions for new ones. Creation in destruction, she would say to them, life amidst death.

She thought they would be safe enough to sit under trees.

There is the burning in her lungs again. She finds she cannot imagine the child in this. Locked inside when even the air inside is turning unbreathable, when there is no escape, no respite, from any of it. She doesn't know how to keep a child safe in poison air, not when the neighbors just across the county line are evacuating, not in the knowledge that, they too, one day, might have to run. But where do you run when the whole earth is burning?

Liam stirs from the bed, waking to see her standing there, looking out.

"Morning," he murmurs. Is she imagining it, or does his voice sound scratchy with smoke?

Her body is alien to her. Slow and bloated. She doesn't know if it's the smoke or the shots or both that makes her body feel like it isn't part of her anymore, as if she is simultaneously stuck in it and floating outside it. She imagines the frozen embryos, all curled up like bulbs longing for spring. She tries to imagine the child curled up among them: sleeping and waiting to wake. She cannot find them there. She tries. She searches her imagination, tries to conjure the feeling of them, that child she will carry and hold and help grow, that child who will play under that tree. They aren't there. All she feels is the burning of smoke in her lungs. She knows what it's made of: remnants of forest, dead bodies of trees, of saplings, of seeds, whole landscapes burned into ashes. The grief and the fear and the anger.

"What if we didn't?" she hears herself asking Liam as he sits up in bed. She is not looking at him. She is still looking out, staring down that terrifying sun. She does not want to see her husband's face.

"What?" he asks.

"What if we didn't have a child?"

She is not saying the words, she thinks. The words are saying her.

"Jo—"

"I don't think I want to anymore," the words come out quickly now. She can't hold them back. "Not in this."

She doesn't turn around, but she can hear Liam's silence. She can hear the words he is holding inside him. She hears him rise from the bed, and at first, she thinks he is coming over to her, that he will wrap his arms around her and tell her everything will be alright, that he will say he supports her whatever she chooses, that he will love her anyway. But he doesn't. She hears his footsteps leave the room, move down the hall. She hears him close his office door. She hears the silence that follows. It frightens her more than anything else. She thinks she knows what he will do later. This afternoon, perhaps, or this evening. She thinks she knows what he will say when he collects himself. That it is a difficult time, a time that does terrible things to the mind. That maybe they just need to wait. After the smoke clears and things go back to normal. Try another month. Give her body more time to rest between all the hormones. Talk to the doctor about some alternatives. Maybe try that more natural cycle option that has fewer shots. She thinks she knows he will sound rational, steady, certain. She thinks she knows she will probably agree. She will probably say, yes, let's just take some time. But she also knows, deep inside, that time will not fix it, will not fix her, will not fix a world falling fast into ending, will not fix how deeply she's failed.

She still wants him to try. She still wants those words.

But now, there is only the gray and the sun brooding through it. Now, there is the night no moon can shine through. Now, there is silence between them.

Part Two

Totality

1

Jo drives through the rain. She leaves the windows down so she can smell it, welcoming the wet. It's three days since her last shot; two days since the dry of the weather broke, washing the smoke from the air, giving firefighters across the northwestern part of the state a chance to contain the conflagrations; one day since she told Liam she was taking a week off from work to vacation on her own. "Just to drive somewhere. Not far. Maybe the coast. I think I just need a little time," she told him. "It's been a lot."

He nodded as if he understood, as if he was trying to be understanding. But she heard the edge in his voice, of fear or annoyance or hurt or anger—she couldn't tell—when he said, "We won't see the eclipse together."

She muttered, guiltily, about the likelihood of clouds. She didn't meet his eyes when she said, "It's only a week," and promised to talk more when she returned.

But a part of her mind knew there was a break here. There would be a before and an after. She would not be the same across the divide of them. She dismissed it as a response to the fires, the hormones, the all of it. But it stayed there, quiet, murmuring, maybe. She didn't tell Liam about Ness. And he never asked if she wanted him to come with her.

Now, as she drives, she keeps glancing into her rearview mirror, catching the edge of the rolled-up painting in the back seat. She wonders what Ness will be like now. Will she have the same expressions, the same ways of moving? Of course, she will be older. Jo can imagine the way the lines on her face will have formed: the thousand smiles etched around the corners of her mouth, the furrow in her brow where she always forms her frowns. Jo wonders if the long waves of her hair will have begun to gray yet or if she will have started dying them. Perhaps, she will have cut the hair all off.

Jo tried looking her up online before leaving but she found very little, and no pictures of Ness herself. Just a few notes about gallery shows and an online shop selling her paintings. Jo scrolled through the paintings, trying to discern how much Ness's work had changed. She thinks it has grown darker and more mysterious, the vibrant yellows and oranges and reds shifting to deep blues and greens, the wild shapeshifting women replaced with the more abstract underwater play of current and shadow. The web page held rivers and oceans wrought in oils. It whirled with waves.

And then there were the selkies. Stylized multi-panel paintings telling the stories of seal-women caught on land. Close up studies of what hid inside their deep sad eyes, their silver fur.

"My family has a selkie in it," Ness told her once. "So many greats ago we've lost count."

Ness laughed when she said it, that light bubbling sound that always made Jo's breath catch in her throat. But inside the laugh, there was something more, something secret and serious.

In Jo's memory, Ness so often eludes her like that. She can never hold her clear and certain.

2

Each day, her hands were stained a different hue. The first day Jo saw her, they were streaked the colors of violets and moss. The first day she spoke to her, really spoke to her, her fingers were bright with red and orange and gold as she dropped the coins into Jo's hand over the register and briefly brushed her palm.

Jo had been haunting the campus coffee shop. Every morning at the same time, right before her classes, for a week she'd come, pulled by the gravitational potential of seeing the woman with the rainbow hands. Jo would stammer out a coffee order, caught by the watery grayblue of her eyes, and watch as she poured the coffee into the white ceramic mug and handed it across the counter. Jo would hand her the bills. The woman would hand back the coins. The exchange felt electric in its absence of touch. A moment of pause. Coffee steam curling between them. Then nothing. Jo would pick up the mug, tell herself not to drop it, drop it, drop it, and take her usual seat by the window. Jo would sit with her back to the counter, imagining she could feel the cool of the woman's stare on the back of her neck. She'd wrap her hands around the mug the woman's hands had touched. She'd drink the coffee the woman had poured for her. She'd feel the coins in her pocket. She would not spend them. She would set them on her desk in her room. Glints of silvery nickels and dimes. Tiny piles of pennies. Jo would glance at them as she wrote, watch for words to spark off them. She'd discovered a currency of poetry.

On the first day they spoke—spoke beyond the usual coffee shop pleasantries—Jo surprised herself and found her voice. They'd just completed the usual "good morning" "howareyou" "fine" "smallcoffeeplease" "hereyougo" "thanks" "enjoy."

"Do you paint?" Jo heard herself asking, wanting to keep the woman's eyes on her for just a moment longer.

Jo watched the blush creep into the woman's cheeks and felt a strange power there— she'd made her blush—until she felt her own blush rise to meet it.

The woman frowned her confusion.

"Your hands," Jo explained. The awkward giggle began to bubble from her throat, caught at the back of her tongue, came out strangled.

The woman didn't seem to notice. "Art major," she said, looking at her fingers in surprise, as if she hadn't ever realized how easily they could give her away.

Jo nodded.

Together, they made a word-seeking pause. Jo found hers first.

"What are you working on now?"

"Portraits," she said. "Sort of."

"Sort of?"

That's when the woman's words began to fall like undammed water and Jo finally exhaled her held breath. "Women shapeshifting," she said. All based on real people she knew. She'd begin painting them like regular portraits, then she'd let the women change under her brush. "They turn into pieces of nature: plants, animals, rocks. I think it'll end up being a series. It's all very mythological ecofeminist. That sort of thing."

"You don't know what they'll turn into when you start?" Jo asked.

She shook her head. "I follow the paint." She said the words seriously. Then she laughed at herself. "I know. That sounds silly."

"No," Jo said, "it doesn't."

And then, Jo shocked herself with her daring. "I'm a poet. So, I kind of get what you mean. I think."

Jo had never said it out loud before, never claimed it like this, so boldly, to a stranger. She wanted to meet the woman's eyes when she said it, to see her reaction, to see whether she believed her or laughed at the statement. But she couldn't. Her eyes fell to the counter between them.

"I'm Ness, by the way," she heard the woman say, holding her hand out to Jo. They shook over the counter. Fingers touched palms, wrapped around them, the whole encounter turned suddenly delicate, as if any wrong motion could break it.

In the long pause that followed, Jo thought that that might be it. That they'd lose the thread of this thing they were beginning to weave together, that she'd be too embarrassed, now, to come back again tomorrow, that she wouldn't have the courage to speak again. Then something in Ness's expression changed, solidified, a resolve.

"I usually go walk by the river on my lunch break. If you want to come?" she asked.

Jo nodded, managed the one word, "Yes."

"I love the river. I think she's my favorite part of living here."

"She," Jo repeated, enchanted.

"Sailors used to call the ocean *she*, like the ocean was a creature with her own will. *It* just doesn't seem right for a river."

Jo nodded. She understood. She could never bear to call an animal or insect or plant or tree *it*, always cringed a little when she had to, as if she'd shorn a part of their livingness away with two sharp letters.

"My break's at one," Ness said.

"I'll come back right after class," Jo told her, reminded, suddenly, of time and how late she was running.

On the way out, Jo pushed the door instead of pulling and tried to pretend Ness was not watching her mistake even as she felt her eyes on her. She willed her feet to walk, one and then the other, not to trip or fall, as she met the chill of the early spring air. She did not look back, then. Not once.

3

"You're writing in watercolors when you should be writing in oils."

Jo could hardly concentrate in class, even as her poem was critiqued. She moved her pen over her notebook, trying to take useful notes, but thinking only of Ness, of the river, of the way she could still feel the ghost of Ness's palm in her hand. She was watching for the clock to tick one.

The professor's words jarred her back to herself. They caught somewhere inside her, and she knew they would echo for a long time after, longer, most likely, than the professor himself would remember them.

She almost laughed when she heard the beginning of his critique. That he would use a painting metaphor, today of all days. But he continued. Her poems, he said, needed more embodiment. They were too wispy, too fragile. Weak. Her classmates agreed. One of them told her he wanted "more blood on the page," and everyone nodded as if they, too, wanted blood.

She tried, dutifully, to record their comments in her notebook, reminding herself this course was meant to be an ordeal, a rite of passage. "Survive this and your poetry can survive anything," one of her friends who took the class the year before had told her. The professor's style was known for being tough and everyone said the students respected him for it. They appreciated his honesty. They knew it was good for them. But, just last week, Jo had stumbled on a girl crying in the bathroom after her poems were called overwrought and "purple as heliotrope."

It wasn't hard for Jo to see her poems the way her workshop did. She knew they were wispy. She feared they were too light, so rarely holding more than images and impressions. They weren't weighty poems. They weren't serious poems. They weren't full of meaning and experience. But, sometimes, she liked their lightness, the way the words felt heady and ethereal in her hands as she wrote them down, catching them as best she could, before they floated on. She was always surprised, as she wrote, by what a poem became. She never knew what she was writing until she got to the end of it. It felt, sometimes, like the poems wrote her, shaping the routes her mind took. She'd be looking at the steam rising out of her coffee and then, a poem would come, and suddenly the steam would change, become the mist of a memory of winter walks, visibly exhaling. And, afterward, the coffee would always breathe for her.

"They're beautiful words," the professor was saying, wrapping up as the clock ticked to 12:50. "Of course. You wouldn't have gotten into this class if they weren't. But words need substance."

"Thank you," Jo said into the silence at the workshop's end, smiling, nodding to the room, her hand shaking a little as she held the pen over the page. "That was all so helpful."

4

Jo was late getting back to the coffee shop. Ness was late getting off her shift. When they finally got to the river, out where the gray clouds and gray water met the yellow daffodils and bright green leaves of spring, it felt like a triumph.

On that first walk, Ness talked mostly of her painting.

"There are all these myths, you know," she said, "where people turn into animals or trees or stones or stars or mountains. I think those stories are trying to tell us something."

"That we need to be closer to nature?"

"Well, sure, but more than that. Like, maybe," Ness paused, looking around her. Jo could hear the breeze moving through the new leaves above them, the water rushing in the river below, the birds and the laughter of a group of students rounding the curve of the path. "Maybe, the moss on this tree, here. The way we see it as so much apart from ourselves, like a whole different creature, maybe that's wrong. Maybe we're closer than we know."

Jo gazed at the moss, the bright green of it, how it almost glowed in the muted spring sunlight. She wasn't really sure she understood what Ness was trying to tell her, but she also thought that, maybe, she did. She reached her fingers out to the moss at the base of the tree, imagining the deep green could feel her touch. For a moment, she could almost perceive the moss reaching back. She smiled up at Ness.

"Soft," Jo said.

Ness laughed. Her laugh echoed the sounds of the river.

After that first time, they met to walk by the river almost every day.

5

Jo started reading Greek myths, searching for substance. In the library, she sat with gods and goddesses, heroes and maidens and monsters. One afternoon, her mind caught on Daphne, the tree-girl, a nymph running from Apollo, turned to a tree by a river god to make an escape. It was a sad story, frightening, but also, Jo thought, the kind of myth that feels true in a slantwise sort of way.

She tried to start a poem right there at the library table, book open for reference, but the words felt stuck inside her, twisted as they tried to get out, dusty and dead when they landed on the page.

6

On their next walk, Jo and Ness paused under a willow on the riverbank. Just off the path, they were hidden beneath a fall of leaves when they kissed, caught in this other world that sat adjacent to the one they left.

Their lips met in a hairfall of wild water, root angle in a rush of currents catching sun, soft invasion of tongue. Rough of bark to hold when knees began to buckle. Whisper of willow. Then. Sensation of roots growing down, branching out.
Blood turned to water   running   impossibly   upward
transformation-willow-river-girl
boundaried broken rush into each other
     earthsky
        landwater
         leafskin
When Ness pulled herself back, her eyes were oceans.

They did not speak. Jo didn't know a language, could not find the words to make containers.

Back on the path, they walked with fingers
               interlocking,
                not wanting to
              untouch.

7

Sex with Ness felt
        like being unmade.
    At first, Jo found her own shape heightened. She had never,
she thought, experienced her own form more clearly than
she did when Ness brushed the skin of her thighs with her
palm, faced the bone of her hip with her nose, mouth, tongue.
Then, a strange
            dissolve,
                a falling
                and a falling
                                apart,
a tumbling off of the world.
Or deeper into it.
    Afterward, she could never tell if the self in Ness's arms was
the same self that had started it or if it was a wholly unique
creation, newly born and held awake.

8

On their first morning, Jo saw the women covering Ness's walls. Sunlight filtered through the window, glancing off the painted shape changers: women half enclosed inside sealskins, women with antlers, women baring the faces of wolves. They didn't seem frozen, the way people in paintings usually did. They didn't seem still at all. They seemed to shift as she watched them and she felt convinced that, if she watched them for long enough, she'd catch them in the midst of movement.

She didn't know how long she'd been staring when she felt Ness move besides her. Ness was not quite awake yet. Her hair fanned out over the pillow like a dreamer pulled out of a fairy tale. She lay on her back, hugging herself with her arms, her face turned away and toward the light of the window.

When Ness finally opened her eyes, Jo felt the strong tug of currents, as if she'd stumbled into the pull of deep water. Ness blinked at her and propped her head up on her hand, still surfacing. Jo wondered what dreams clung to her, imagined she could almost see them, a soft web of netting glistening in the morning sun.

"They're beautiful," Jo said, gesturing to the paintings.

Ness smiled.

"What do they mean?" The words came out blunt and wrong.

Ness laughed, her eyes still blinking between waking and sleep.

"What does anyone mean by anything?" she asked, and her voice sounded far away, echoing back from wherever she'd been in the night.

Jo shook her head.

Ness drew her brows together. The expression gave her face a surprising seriousness, as if she had grown twenty years in a moment, as if there was an old woman lurking under her young skin.

"One of my professors said it was about masks, about the selves we wear for others and the selves we really are. But I don't think that's it."

"What do you think?"

Ness pursed her lips, seeking words. "I think it's really about changing shape. How no shape is ever entirely stable. How we all can, at any moment, in an instance, shift."

"Shift?" Jo asked, surprised by the quick intimacy, by the sense that Ness was sharing her philosophy of life on their first morning together.

Ness shrugged. "I don't think I can explain it any better in words. Maybe that's why I keep trying to paint it."

9

She put it in a poem, that first kiss.

She went back to the riverbank to write under the tree.

Sitting beneath the willow, her back against the bark, she remembered the brush of Ness's breath on her cheek, that uncertain moment before their lips met, the way the river rushed in, and the trees. Further down the bank, she saw a birch slanting toward the water. The tree looked like a woman in flight, caught in a moment of bark as she moved toward the current. Running away? Or running toward something? Jo scrambled down the banks. That running. That feeling of fast shift through air before feet dug to ground, before lungs' last human breath and the limbs growing skyward. Jo put her ear against the bark and heard a heartbeat, the rhythms of the poem there, steadfast, bright as a hummingbird buzz. What if she saw the change coming? What if she ran so it couldn't catch her—or so she could catch it faster? The poem lived in the tree at that uncertain angle, not yet settled into shape, knowing, at any moment, the form could change again.

Her professor called it "strange but interesting." Her classmates said the "Classical references felt derivative, but the images were fresh."

Jo kept going back to the river to write.

10

It wasn't until the third night they spent together that Ness asked to paint Jo.

In Ness's room, they'd turned out all the lights, but the moon was shining in, casting a silvery glow over the bed. All they could see was each other.

Ness was tracing the curve of Jo's hip, making her feel exposed and self-conscious and thrilled beneath her gaze that did not waver, but pushed past discomfort, seeking depths. An artist's gaze, Jo thought. Or a lover's.

"What creature do you want to turn me into?" Jo asked.

"I don't know yet," Ness said, studying her jaw line, the curve of her chin. "I can't tell what you'll become in the paint."

Jo couldn't see the paintings on the walls in the dark, but she could sense the women-creatures staring down at them. She wondered how many had shared this bed with Ness before becoming a part of her collection.

"Why me?" Jo asked.

"Because there's something inside you," Ness said, studying her hands now, running eyes over palms, tracing the bones of the fingers, "that I want to pull out."

11

Jo didn't notice, at first, the pursuing sound of wings. It wasn't until the birds began to call to each other that she looked up. There, perched on the wires, were three crows, cawing and flapping. As they walked, the crows swooped down toward them and then back up to perches nearer by, shadowing from above.

"Are those crows following us?" Jo asked, laughing at the ridiculousness of her question.

"Yeah," Ness said, "they do that to me sometimes."

Her voice sounded half embarrassed and half proud.

"They're harmless," she added, seeing Jo's nervous glances up. "They only really dive-bomb in fledgling season."

"Why," Jo asked, "do they follow you?"

Ness shrugged.

"I don't know. At first, I thought maybe I'd offended them somehow. You know, they have a really good memory for faces. If you cross a crow, you can have generations of trouble with them. But they aren't actually aggressive, really. I mean, right now, you see they aren't trying to chase us away or anything. They're just coming along. Sometimes I wonder if they might be trying to tell me something."

"What do you think they're trying to say?"

Ness sighed. "I wish I knew."

Jo looked up again at the birds in all their avian mystery.

She could see their dark eyes glinting down as they perched, watchful and entirely unreadable.

Eventually, Jo came to realize it wasn't just the crows that circled Ness. It was everyone. Ness was naturally magnetic. The neighborhood cats, for instance, found her irresistible. Whenever Jo walked to campus with Ness, she'd have to make sure they left early so Ness could greet all the felines on their route as the animals appeared, emerging from cat doors and driveways, coming out from under bushes, to rub against her legs. At parties, Ness could always be found with the cat or dog of the house, petting the creature as she held court with the many human friends and acquaintances who would hover around her all night.

Jo did love, in some ways, at first, the going to parties with Ness. Those initial minutes when they walked in together and Ness introduced her as "my poet girlfriend," casually draping an arm over her shoulder like Jo belonged there. Belonged to her.

But, as the night wore on, more and more people would crowd between them until Ness seemed to forget about her entirely and Jo would end up sitting in a corner being talked at by some English major guy wanting to explain to her about the brilliance of Hemingway while she sipped her beer and tried not to look bored.

Eventually, Jo would slip away. She'd skirt to the edges of things, then drift outside to the porch and down the steps to a nearby tree where she'd pause to breathe into the quiet moonlight and dissolve into the sense of escape. She'd watch the noisy groups walk by and wonder what it might be like to actually *like* parties, to find energy in them, to look forward to them.

Sometimes Jo thought what she really loved most about going to parties with Ness was the walking home alone. Being out deep in the night. The way the wind sounded then, as it moved through the branches of trees. The things she could sense when the human world had finally gone quiet. Sometimes, on those late lone walks home, a little tipsy, perhaps a little stoned, she'd be sure she could hear words in that rustling. She'd be convinced the trees were calling to her, were trying to get her a message.

12

Ness started the painting by making a sketch of Jo's face. Jo sat for it one evening, very still by the window, listening to the scratch of the pencil. She thought she could almost feel it, the smooth of the graphite tickling her cheeks, nose, mouth. Her face felt malleable, as if it could move and reshape itself according to the pencil's suggestion. Afterward, she wrote a poem about a woman in a painting who, staring back at herself, could no longer tell how much her self had shaped the painting and how much the painting itself had shaped her. Her writing class almost seemed to like it. The professor told her the poem was fuller than her previous work, that her poetry was progressing.

Ness began the painting the next day, but every time Jo was over, she covered it with a sheet. She wouldn't let her see it until it was finished.

"You need the complete vision," she said. "It won't make sense if you only see a part of it."

So, Jo waited, wondering what animal Ness would turn her into. Would she be a creature of land or water or air? Would she seem fierce or kind or shy or free?

Some days, she thought the painting would reveal a self that only Ness could see, the self she knew herself to be around her: a braver, more expressive self, the self that wrote in oils.

13

Every morning, Jo went to the river to catch the poems. They would come to her slowly, not all at once, not every day, as she wandered the banks or paused beneath trees. They'd start quiet, a rustle like a mouse in the groundcover, almost imperceptible unless her ear was tuned just right, unless her attention was turned to the precise time and place. But then, if she focused, quieting the rest of her, letting the trees and the river and the wind and the plants and the animals trace the shape of her so that her own mind receded, with its buzz of papers and deadlines and parties, to be superseded by something else, another her, a her that was part of the landscape, as belonged to it as a mushroom growing under a leaf, a her that was connected to the whispers of breeze-beloved branches and the murmurings of ground-embraced roots, if she let herself be transformed in this way, she could hear the poems. She could catch them as they came to write them down, almost full and finished.

14

One day, watching Ness sketch, Jo mentioned her professor's paint metaphor, hoping Ness would scoff and reassure her about the watercolors. Instead, Ness frowned, thinking.

"Yeah," she said, finally, "I can see that. You are sort of a watercolor kind of person."

"What do you mean?" Jo asked.

"You kind of disperse," Ness said. "Like when watercolor hits the paper, it sort of bleeds out into it, and the color softens. It's hard to get a really rich color with watercolors. It takes the right attention and technique. But with the right technique, watercolor can do things no other paint can. It's just hard to get it right."

"I disperse?"

Ness sighed, and Jo could tell she was annoyed. "It's like, sometimes, when I'm looking at you, it's as if you start to disappear."

"I don't think I understand."

"I'm just not making sense," Ness said quickly, sharp, but trying now, Jo could tell, to be gentle. "Your professor shouldn't have told you you needed oils. That's silly. You just need to find your technique."

15

It happened the night Ness and her housemates threw a party. It was late spring then. The leaves had turned from pale and tenuous to bold and deeply green.

She recognized the woman from one of Ness's paintings. She couldn't tell how. In the painting her face was blurred, but the feeling was distinctive. In the painting, her short hair turned spiky, and she seemed to hold a determination that unsettled Jo, a strength she could never imagine mustering, as she prickled her way to porcupine.

That night, real and living, the woman caught her staring and smiled.

"You're one of Ness's girls," the woman said.

The phrase startled Jo. It felt so far from what she felt herself to be. *one girl of ness—girls of ness—ness's girls—ness's.* The words buzzed around her brain, reconfiguring themselves. Maybe, she thought, she'd mistaken the meaning.

"You're one of the paintings," Jo stammered, blushing.

"You can tell?" the woman asked, surprised, now, herself.

Jo nodded. "They're really great, aren't they?"

"Definitely," she said. "I've seen them so many times, I usually forget that they're there." She held Jo's gaze as she continued, and Jo felt herself caught in the sharp of her. "Last night, I got startled by the one peering out from the rock. I completely forgot she was right next to the bed." The woman laughed, and her laugh felt sharp too, like a weapon. "*Yours* is interesting," she said.

"Mine?" Jo heard her voice say, though she couldn't feel herself speak the words. In that unsteady moment, before the realization set in, she couldn't feel anything.

"It looks just like you."

This woman had seen her painting. She had been with Ness just the night before.

The woman smiled again. The smile seemed satisfied now. She released Jo's eyes and said goodnight and walked away. But Jo couldn't move. She was frozen in the shock of the cruelty.

Later that night, while Ness was surrounded by friends, forgetting Jo at the edges again, Jo slipped upstairs to her girlfriend's room. She turned on a lamp. There they were, illuminated, all those women changing shape. She wouldn't let herself look at the porcupine. She moved quickly to the sheet, grasped it. She paused. She'd made Ness a promise. It would be a violation of trust. She looked around the room at all the women staring back at her, witnessing. She felt so childish, suddenly, so stupidly naive, so angry with herself and Ness and the porcupine and all the women on the walls. She pulled back the sheet.

It took her a moment to know what she was seeing. At first, it looked only like splotches of white crinkled over with dull oranges and yellows. Then, amidst all the muted colors, she made out the shape of her face and the colors found their sense.

Ness had made her a tree, a birch, pale and peeling, with falling leaves curling away from her. In the painting, her face looked consumed, as if it were shredding itself into tree-stuff. Her eyes, in the painting, were manifold, scars in the bark, dark and strange, enveloped by their irises until they looked hardly human at all. When she looked closer, over and across each piece of peeling bark, in tiny handwriting that looked, at first, like tree matter, she could make out the words of her poems.

When Ness opened the door, Jo was sitting on the bed, still staring at the painting. Ness reached for the sheet Jo still held. Jo grasped it more tightly. She didn't look up, didn't want to see what Ness thought of her. She was surprised when Ness's voice came out quiet and sad, when she said, "You promised you wouldn't look."

Jo saw Ness's face then, the disappointment that went so far down she knew she'd never find the true depths of it. She looked away.

"You showed her," Jo said.

"Who?"

Jo pointed to the painting by the door. "The porcupine."

"I needed an opinion," Ness said. "She's an artist too."

"What did she think?"

"She liked it. She thought I should add more leaves. And the text of your poems. That was her idea. Brilliant."

"You showed her my poems?" Jo asked, horrified, imagining the two of them in this room examining her words, laughing together at the awkward phrasing, the overly earnest lines, the muddled imagery.

"Sure," Ness said. "Why not? She liked them."

"You're sleeping with her," Jo accused, her voice wavering as she said it, uncertain, now, how she should feel, what feelings she should let Ness see.

"Sometimes," Ness said. "I mean, off and on." She made the confession so casually it didn't sound like a confession at all.

"But I thought...." Jo didn't finish the sentence, didn't

know how without sounding silly, didn't want to sound silly, not now.

"We're not exclusive," Ness said. "You don't think we're doing *that*, right?"

Jo didn't know what to say. She was mortified by her own misunderstanding. She'd thought so many things that now, it seemed, she shouldn't have.

"People like us don't think they own each other like that," Ness said.

"People like us."

Jo felt herself receding, moving inward to a place where there was no voice to speak from. She handed the sheet back to Ness and walked toward the door.

"The painting," Ness called after her. "You like it, right?"

Jo looked back then and saw how Ness wavered, saw how she could hurt her if she wanted to. She paused, and in that pause, Ness shifted again, made an elegant little snarl with her mouth and upturned eyebrow. "I mean, you get it, right?"

Jo felt the sting but also the power of the conversation they were having beneath the words, the arguments they were making, the vulnerabilities they were trying to hide from each other.

"Yes," Jo said. She kept her voice even and clear, perhaps a little cold, trying, now, not to give too much away. "It's very *obvious*."

16

They didn't talk about it after. But something had changed. Jo couldn't find the words for it, though she tried, this distance between them that seemed new but might simply have been newly noticed. Perhaps, Jo thought, they had always been this far away from each other.

The painting disappeared from Ness's room and when Jo mustered the courage to ask about it, a week later, Ness told her she'd taken it to the campus art studio.

"It's almost done," she said, not meeting Jo's eyes. "It's just easier to finish it there."

17

The first time was an accident. Ness was talking to her house-mate in the kitchen while Jo studied in her room. She was holding the highlighter above her textbook and, when it fell from her hand, it made a tiny bright yellow dot on a painting that was propped up against the desk. The dot was so small it was almost invisible. You had to know just where to look, and look closely, to find it. When she saw it, Jo was horrified. But then, past the horror, the thrill that came from marking. However subtly, however near invisibly, she'd changed Ness's work. It was altered now, forever.

The next time, she did it on purpose, with a pencil, thinking that would be less permanent, a test run. She found a tiny gray corner of another painting and drew a line. It squiggled over the brush strokes, small and unobtrusive.

After that, she started using Ness's paints. She'd wait until Ness left the room to shower or make coffee. Then she'd find whatever color was left out and use it. She grew bolder with each stroke. Always a little hopeful she'd be caught. She wondered if Ness would be able to tell which strokes in the paintings were hers. She wondered, if she ever found them, if she'd suspect Jo, or if she'd think it was another lover.

18

At the end of the spring, as finals were finishing, Ness invited Jo on a trip to the coast.

"Just you and me and the ocean," she said, "if you want?"

Ness sounded uncharacteristically tentative when she asked. Jo hadn't seen her like this before, so disarmingly nervous. She was charmed. It was almost, Jo thought, like an apology. It was almost a kind of an offering.

"Where exactly?" Jo asked.

Ness told her the story. Her grandfather had, decades back, bought a tiny, run-down bed and breakfast, always intending to fix it up but never quite managing it.

"My grandparents even retired to it for a while before my grandpa died and my grandma went into the care home. It's pretty old and run down, but really great."

Ness wasn't meeting her eyes. She was looking past her into some anxious middle distance of embarrassment.

"Okay," Jo heard herself say. "I'd love to come."

Ness's smile looked like genuine relief and Jo realized Ness had been afraid she'd say no.

The possibility of no didn't cross Jo's mind until later when she realized the trip would mean she had to take time off from her job at the campus bookstore, that she didn't know how long Ness was planning for, that she, herself, didn't have a car so she'd be relying on Ness to drive them out and back to a place she didn't know. It disturbed her, then, the amount of trust she'd be placing in Ness, how uncertain she felt about the wisdom of it.

19

They set out on the last day of finals, driving past the bars that were fast filling with celebratory students, past the dorms where freshmen packed boxes into cars, past the student houses where kegs and beer pong tables sprung up in preparation for the night of parties. The sky was full of clouds, a gray backdrop to all the bright activity. Soon, they'd left the town behind entirely, making for forest.

The way the mist hung about the trees, drifting in and out of branches, turning the colors of the woods a muted green and gray, made the drive feel mysterious, like a journey to a world outside the world. They set out in the morning, when the roads were empty, and the clouds were just beginning to glow a strange suncast silver. It had rained the night before, and the streets all glistened wet.

They were quiet as they went, driving west, Ness at the wheel. Jo couldn't tell if the silence was awkward or comfortable. As they moved from city to forest, the journey pulled her out of herself. Having left the familiar, she couldn't seem to find internal bearings.

The firs were crowding the highway, as if they had only just stepped aside for a moment to make way and could shift back any time, flooding the road with their shadows, plunging them into deep forest.

20

"My grandparents brought my mom and her brothers here every summer," Ness said as they climbed the creaking porch steps and unlocked the blue door. "Then, when I was growing up, we all came back every June. Sometimes I'd stay here with my grandparents until school started up again. It was perfect. Just this big old house and the ocean and the trees and the gulls."

"Does your family still come back here much?" Jo asked. Ness had gotten the door open after a struggle with the lock. Inside, the house smelled musty. The surfaces held a silver layer of dust.

"Not much. My parents were renting it out for a while, but that's a lot of trouble, so now they just have me drop by to check on things every few months."

The floorboards creaked with every step, echoing into the empty house with eerie reverberations. It felt, Jo thought, like the house was speaking to them. She watched a spider scurry across the floor, disturbed by the new human presence.

Ness stood in the entryway and sighed.

"I love this place. I'm going to live here one day."

The living room was already set up with paints and canvas, everything left out as if someone had just gone out for a walk and would be back momentarily. But they glinted with the same sheen of dust.

"When were you last here?" Jo asked.

"Winter."

Ness had moved into the kitchen, taking stock of the cupboards, more at ease, Jo realized, than she had ever seen her. Jo thought back to the winter, all the times Ness had disappeared for a day or a week, unreachable by phone, unfindable at all their usual spots. She wondered if this is where Ness had been, and she felt a moment of jealousy, sharp in her chest, a resentment for this house that had taken Ness away from her.

But now, Ness was making two mugs of tea and beckoning her over to the kitchen table, telling her stories of childhood summers.

Jo was astonished at how much Ness revealed of herself in this place. She'd learned more about her past in these first few minutes than she had in all the months they'd been dating. Ness even looked different here. Something had relaxed inside her, leaving her surfaces visibly softened. Here, Ness had a vulnerability Jo felt a new rising urge to protect.

21

On each of her hands, between her middle and ring fingers, Ness held matching scars. Jo had never asked about them, had never wanted to let Ness know she'd noticed them. But here, in this house, Ness showed them to her, unembarrassed.

"My selkie scars," Ness said, holding her hands up with her fingers spread apart as if fingers themselves were a wonder.

"My grandma," she continued. "That's who I get them from. But it probably goes farther back than that. Legend has it that children with selkie blood have webbed fingers at birth. It's called simple syndactyly now. The word literally means together fingers."

She held her two fingers against each other, disappearing the space between them, to demonstrate.

"They did the surgery when I was a baby, so I don't remember. But Grandma always said it was her selkie blood come through."

The scars were silverwhite like the glint of the moon on the sea.

"It's a story in my family. Kind of a legend. That we had a selkie, once, so many greats ago no one can count them. The man saw her woman-shaped on the shore and found her skin and hid it and married her and they had kids."

Jo knew selkie stories. She knew how they so often ended.

"Did she ever find it again," Jo asked, "her skin? Or did it stay hidden forever?"

"I don't know. No one ever told me."

Jo tried to imagine it, the hidden part of a self, the finding or not finding it. The terrible choice. To stay or to go. The irresistible pull of the water. The children standing on the shore, watching their mother return to the waves, watching her change back into herself and leave them.

"I saw this seal once, up north, in the Sound. The seal swam right up to me and met my eyes and stared, like she had something to tell me. A secret held between us. I don't know what. I couldn't stop shivering, the look she gave me."

"When?" Jo asked. She couldn't see Ness's face clearly, but the tone of her voice had gone distant, far away into a memory that ran so deep she could hardly name it.

"Oh, a long time ago," she said. "I must have been ten or eleven. I tried to paint the seal once, but I couldn't get the shape right."

Ness tried to laugh, but the sound caught and came out tentative. Whatever look the seal had given her, whatever feeling she got from it, whatever that look woke, was still hiding inside her. Jo wondered how well it was hidden. She wondered if Ness even saw it herself.

Jo reached for her hands, interlocked their fingers, imagining the thresholds they carried. She imagined a woman who was also a seal who was also a woman.

In the future, far from this moment, when there is the child, when the child asks about their own scars, Jo will give the story.

"They're from her," she will say, "from your other mom."

Proof, she will not say but she will think, each and every time, that you are hers and mine together.

22

They set out for ocean early in the morning, just as the sun was beginning to lighten the clouds. They walked down the block, turned three corners, and came to the place where the road ended in sand dunes. The tide was out, and the water looked soft in the tidepools, glistening velvet. Out of the pools rose the stumps of ancient trees, like standing stones covered in sea-stuff.

"Welcome to the ghost forest," Ness said.

Jo had never heard the term before, had never seen anything like these petrified arboreal memories. The tidepools caught their reflections and sunk them down like doubles, sylvan twins above and below.

"They're all up and down the coast. Some are from the last big earthquake when the land fell into the sea and dropped the trees into the water. Some are way older than that. Those were made slower by the gradual rise of the ocean, the saltwater getting into their roots and poisoning them."

"Which are these?" Jo asked.

"I don't know," Ness said. "I think the scientists are still debating."

Jo felt afraid to touch them. They seemed angry in their deathly dreaming, spiking with limpets and anemone, alive and haunting. They seemed, Jo thought, not just like monuments of long past catastrophe, but like memories of future destruction. She felt a convergence of time tangling up and wondered if that was apocalypse, when all the boundaries broke, and time circled back on itself.

"Aren't they beautiful?" Ness asked.

23

They spent the afternoon drinking coffee and reading, calling out quotes across the porch. For dinner, they made brownies with too much chocolate, licking the batter from each other's fingers as the pan baked. Ness opened a bottle of cheap red wine that stained their teeth and they lay in the grass in the backyard listening to the sounds of the waves. Jo glowed beneath the vast gray of the sky, beside the wilds of water.

That night, skin to skin, they slept, and Jo saw what they were making here. A temporary cove. A world just off the world. Small and strange and warm. In the tangle they made of their bodies, Jo dreamed trees

    inundated leaves stripped in the currents, whirling to
    root to ocean
    dark at the depths, bright sharp of silver
    glint beneath seafloor, soft as the echo
    of waves, this newness born
    of submersion

In the midst of the dream, Jo woke halfway, Ness shifting in her sleep, hair tickling her collarbone, the smooth of her cheek at her throat.

24

Morning. Jo woke with a poem in her head. She reached for her notebook, scribbled quick, eyes still dream-blurred. She tried to catch the words, but they were slippery, sliding as she struggled to pin them to page with only pencil. She knew she was done when a blank feeling fell over her and her mind rested empty for a moment. All the words she hadn't caught had flown, lost to her forever. Only then did she notice the rumpled blankets in the bed beside her. Ness was already up. Jo put the notebook aside. She'd look at it later, decide what was really salvageable from that half-dreaming space.

The house was still dark, floorboards creaking as she walked. Jo thought she saw, flitting through the shadows as she moved down the stairs, Ness as a child. Barefoot and running across the hall. Maybe houses held memories, replayed them the way humans did, caught on certain moments, certain images or feelings or words, for no particular reason except that they'd become, somehow, a part of the fundamental material that made up the heart of them.

Jo wondered if the house would remember her presence, would replay this week the way she knew that she would, or if she would just be one fleeting moment in the long life of the place, hardly noticed and easily forgotten.

She found Ness in the living room, sketching. Ness looked up when the floor creaked, then moved her eyes back to paper.

"I woke up with an image," Ness told her. "I didn't want to disturb you."

"I woke with a poem," Jo said, thinking her voice still sounded like sleeping, somehow both a part of and apart from her body.

Ness smiled. "This place is like that. It always gives me dreams."

"Can I see yours?"

Ness added a last line before turning the sketchpad around so she could see. There, penciled out, was the underwater tree from Jo's dream. It was differently angled, all distinctly in Ness's style, but all the parts were there: the currents, the stripped leaves, the solid weathering trunk, the glinting roots. It was like seeing her own dream through Ness's eyes.

Ness frowned. "You hate it."

"I dreamed it. Exactly. That's exactly the tree from my dream."

"Really?"

Jo nodded. Ness smiled, the anticipating smile of someone on the brink of discovery.

"Your poem."

Her poem.

Jo ran upstairs, almost tripping on the last step, to get her notebook. She could hardly remember what she'd written. She brought it downstairs, taking the steps two at a time, handed the open notebook to Ness and read over her shoulder.

They both stared at the poem for a long time before looking back at each other.

"Wow," Ness said. "We had the same dream."

"How?"

"I told you this house was magic."

There was something moving through the air between

them, a current that pulled. Jo knew they both felt it, this strange sense of mind touching mind. Like a tiny muscle she never knew existed until it moved itself, the source of the feeling was utterly unlocatable.

They were kissing, then, and Ness was pulling off her t-shirt. Jo was moving on top of her, pressing herself against her, feeling animal. But even as they wrapped themselves up in each other, they could not get close enough. The vibrations of bodies, all the shifting skin and bones, got in the way.

25

It was the same the next night and the next—a dream, a sketch, a poem pulled from the space before waking.

Soon they were both waking in the middle of the night, writing and painting in the dark, possessed by the same visions. Trees and water. Ocean forests. Seals and gulls and crows. The borderlands of shore and sea. The flood that comes upending.

They worked almost without thinking, elemental, passing notes and sketches back and forth, shifting them, changing and revising words and lines, trying ways to weave the forms together. For some, Jo wrote her poems on the canvases before Ness painted over them, the words secreted beneath the image. They tried scraping away some of the paint on a few, letting select words peek through, hinting at the more underneath. Jo tried writing them on the backs of the canvases, in the corners, along the sides. For some, Ness's earlier method worked, incorporating the words directly into the image like she had with the tree. Beneath Ness's brush, words became water, wind, cloud, sky, bark, leaf, feather, fur.

Jo felt dizzy, watching the retranslations, the words she'd chosen to describe the images turning into the images themselves, the dreams filtered through their two perspectives, the way they saw them different yet the same. Looking at the paintings, it was as if she was catching someone else's memory mingling with her own. It became difficult to tell where each vision ended and the other began. There was always a point for each paintingpoem where it became impossible to know, even in her own mind, which vision was hers.

Jo found Ness sitting in a pool of moonlight with what looked like a blanket in her lap. At first, Ness didn't see her. She was turned toward the window and her face did not look like Ness's face, not the Ness Jo knew. Her eyes glinted silver, and she seemed like something pulled out of a dream, edges blurring out of the world, a being apart from waking.

When she saw Jo, the strangeness broke, and she snapped back to herself with a laugh. She held up the blanket. "My selkie skin," she said.

"Your what?"

She beckoned Jo to come and sit beside her and Jo did, like a child come to hear a story. She leaned her head on Ness's shoulder and looked down at the thing in her arms. Close up, the blanket became not a blanket, but something more like clothing. It had a hood and arms and legs. It was made of velvet, soft and shiny and gray. The inside was a messy quilt of mismatched fabric, all shapes and sizes and colors.

"I made it when I was a kid. When I heard the family stories. At first, I think it was a game, like pretend or imaginary friends. You see, in the stories, the kids of a selkie and their kids and their kids, they're drawn to the water, but they don't have a selkie skin. They were all born human. So, I thought, what if they made their own? I took some of my mom's old fabric. It's a mess. I didn't really know how to sew then. But, inside, that's the magic part, I took all these old family rel-ics—my grandma's handkerchief, a piece of my grandpa's old shirt, one of my mom's dishtowels. I went around, for a while, trying to steal strands of everyone's hair to use as thread. Of course, it always broke. And I kept working on it for, I don't know, it must have been a whole year, just adding pieces and pieces. Then, when we were here that summer, I put it on and went down to the water. I'm not sure what I thought would happen. Maybe that some long lost seal relative would rec-ognize me and come tell me a secret or something. I waded in up to my waist. I remember the water was cold but that didn't really bother me. I had this thought, more than a thought, deeper than that, almost a knowing, that if I really went into the water, all the way, just letting it take me over, I'd change somehow. Like there was a space where I'd meet the water and the water would meet me. Like the ocean inside me would find some outward expression. I hesitated. Just standing there, not knowing what to do next. And this cur-rent caught my legs and pulled me down and tumbled me all the way under the water. And, before it tossed me back to the shore, I felt something. I'm not really sure how to explain it. Like a shift, like something inhuman in me woke up."

The words stopped. Ness looked down at the fabric in her arms and laughed. A nervous laugh? Jo wondered. Or just a sound to break the tension of the words and the silence that followed.

While Ness had been speaking, Jo had felt the rise of her shoulder, the tightening of muscles there.

"I've never told anyone that story," Ness said. "It sounds so crazy when I say it out loud."

"I don't think so," Jo said. She meant it then. Later, she would doubt. Later, she would wonder, after they left the house, the coast, the space between them where the land and sea met, whether she should have felt differently that night, whether she should have said something else, something wiser. But in that moment, in that place between dreaming and waking, she knew Ness was telling her something true in the deepest of ways, was allowing her entry into a secret elemental world that ran beneath the surface of the Ness she knew.

They sat in silence again for a time, looking out the window, watching a cloud pass across the moon, the way the bright shone through the dark haze of it, appeared again, startling and sharp, on the other side.

"How old were you?" Jo asked.

"Oh, really young. Seven? Eight?"

"Were you scared?"

"No. That's the strangest thing about it. I wasn't scared of drowning."

27

The selkie comes into her dreams. Silver-furred and dark-eyed
slips through the water as if
made of water and
the tight grip of current

28

One night, Jo couldn't sleep. The moon was out, full and silver. She walked downstairs and felt herself drawn out the door, down the streets, to the shore. She couldn't see the ghost forest in the height of the tide, but she knew it was there, just under the surface of the water. She could feel the memory of it. She could almost see, beneath the waves, beneath the sand, the stone roots webbing wide. In her mind, they shone like silver, a net that held the whole of the sea. Those old roots, in their deaths, held a message, she was sure, if only she could know how to hear it, if only she could understand the language of their world under the world.

She'd brought her notebook to the shore, but no poems came.

29

That night, the flood came into their dreaming. And they dreamed together, tangled up inside the rush of water, heavy-fast of fate

               felt undertow
   movement cannot be

                  suspension of objects
                   brush and canvas
                      float

   words run over, bleed the paint
                    liquify

                                  the paper

They woke all at once to the sound of rushing water, heavy and pounding like an invasion of strangers. Before Jo could fully open her eyes to the blue glow of predawn, Ness was already running downstairs. She heard the thumps as Ness took them two at a time. Jo ran after her, all the creaks of the floorboard echoing nightmare loud beneath her feet.

At the foot of the stairs, Ness stood, silent, watching the water pool over the living room, floating canvasses and brushes and pencils, drowning the notebooks. Jo couldn't understand what she was seeing. Her first thought was that the ocean had broken into the house, that they had somehow pulled it to them with all their dreaming, that their art-making had created a force to escape the bounds of them. When her waking self came back to her, she knew such things to be impossible. But, even in the future, she will always half believe that that's exactly what caused the flood, that it wasn't the broken old pipe at all, but the ocean itself come to find them.

Ness waded into the water and Jo saw it, for just a moment, through dream-dusted eyes, the silver that webbed over her like a second skin. Like fur. She blinked, and the vision was gone. And it was only Ness again, human and wet, lifting drifting canvases from the water and murmuring, "ruined, ruined."

The plumber came to fix the burst pipe and, after the water drained, they mopped and threw away the sodden mess. They kept the fans going for two days to try to dry it out, to keep the mold from growing behind the walls, under the floorboards. They avoided the living room, mostly stayed upstairs. Downstairs felt like the site of a crime or strange magic, an act of destruction they could not understand but were still, somehow, responsible for.

They left the day before Ness's parents came to survey the damage and see what could be done about the furniture that still smelled of wet. They didn't speak on the drive that was, outside the car, full summer. The sun was bright, but its light seemed weighted and sharp. Jo longed for the quiet of clouds.

"I'm going back out to help my parents," Ness said when she dropped Jo off. "Probably for a week or so. Then I might go back home with them for a bit."

Jo nodded, her mind too fuzzy and tired for words.

"I'll call," Ness promised.

Jo nodded again, stood rooted to the sidewalk until the last glimpse of Ness and her car disappeared around the corner. Even after that, she stood, until the feeling of Ness near had left her, until she knew the sense of separation.

30

In those first weeks without Ness, Jo didn't write a word. The blur of herself moved through days without noticing them. She went to her job at the university bookstore and stood behind the register, staring out at blank space.

Campus had emptied, peopled only with the scant remnants of students taking between-term classes and summer camps renting the empty dorms. Everything felt vague and slow and half unformed.

Ness never called.

Jo had planned to spend the summer writing and working to save money for the following year. She hadn't signed herself up for any classes. But now, she thought, maybe she should have.

The words wouldn't come.

Ness wouldn't call.

The summer blanked with an oppressive emptiness.

<h1 style="text-align:center">31</h1>

That was the summer she met Liam. A friend of a friend introduced them at a party, and at first, Jo tried to keep her distance. She didn't want to lead anyone on.

But then, it was August, and still, Ness hadn't called.

On their first real date, Liam took her to a bar full of old hippies and hip college students. They drank IPAs and ate fried pickles. They sat in a dark corner and held hands over the sticky table and told each other secrets while men with guitars sang softly through the speakers. She could talk to Liam, she realized over the course of that night, like she couldn't talk to anyone else, like she hadn't even been able to talk to Ness.

His hands were larger than hers and his face still seemed hauntingly boyish beneath his stubble. His hair fell over his forehead and, every time he brushed it aside, Jo thought he looked like one of those sensitive brooding guitarists in those bands with heavy slow melodies and lyrics you could whisper back to yourself like poetry. The way he gazed at her made her feel like the most fascinating person in the world, but also as if he could understand her, as if he thought even her edges, her strangenesses, her secret shameful parts, were beautiful.

They went back to his room and opened a bottle of cheap wine and kept talking. She told him about Ness, about how, with her gone, she felt a whole part of herself had been revealed and then stolen away. He talked about following his high school girlfriend to college, about how, then, in the middle of their freshman year, she'd met someone else.

"I thought we'd be together forever," he said in such an earnest tone, she had to take his hand. Then he rolled his eyes at himself. "I know that's ridiculous."

"Not really," she said, "if that's how you felt."

He looked at her a long while then, and she felt time opening between them into a great expanse of possibility.

"Why didn't you transfer?" Jo asked, looking away, suddenly self-conscious.

He shrugged and, with a knowingly mischievous look, he said, "Then I wouldn't have met you."

They both laughed at the line, but she held onto it, turning it over and over all the next week, as if it were a little piece of a destiny, a thread she could follow that might weave into a shape that would hold her.

When they kissed, finally, in the dark depths of the morning, she felt safe, seen. When he took off her clothes, fumbling endearingly with the clasp of her bra, she felt held. Something inside her relaxed and gave in. She cried afterwards, but she couldn't say why. He never asked her, only wiped the tears away as they fell, and she loved him for that.

32

"I need to run an errand," Liam told her, three weeks after their first date at the bar, when she met him after class.

"Oh," she said, disappointed. She'd been looking forward to their date. She'd been anticipating it, she realized, all day. The seeing him. How he would hold her hand in his hand. The way his hand always felt so solid and surprisingly elegant. The little ways that he would find to touch her. Tentative at first, like questions, the hand on her elbow, the brush of his knee against hers. Each date began like this, and then, as the minutes and hours wore on, their bodies would move closer and closer together until she was wrapped up in his arms, her head on his shoulder, his hand moving lightly through her hair.

It was still so early in their dating that he asked before kissing her. She thought that was a sweet and gentle thing. But when they kissed, she could feel an emberring glow between them, slow and steady, moving to ignite.

"I'd love for you to come," he said, now, surprising her, "if you want."

"What's the errand?" she asked, knowing, already, that she would go with him.

He gave her a mysterious grin. "You'll see."

They took the bus from campus. It was late afternoon at summer's end. They watched the languid day edge forward from the windows of the bus. Students relaxed at outdoor tables, enjoying the sunlight, avoiding the heat of the pavement. On the bus, all the windows were open, the warm breeze moving over the seats. She could feel Liam's leg against hers, their bare knees touching. His body had begun to feel familiar beside her. She felt a sense of absence when it was not there.

She still didn't know where they were heading. She thought, at first, they might be going to the mall on the other side of town. But, when they passed by that stop, she wondered what came after. She hadn't ridden the bus line out this far before.

When the bus pulled over into a landscape of parking lots and gray big box stores, Liam stood.

"This is our stop," he said.

He held her hand as he led her over the glare of concrete. The heat rising from the asphalt grew more intense as they walked across the parking lot. The sun glinted from the cars, turning them to strange blurs of light.

She was too distracted by the heat and the sun to look where they were going. So, she was surprised when, having been led through a set of automated sliding doors, she nearly collided with a display of garden hoses.

Liam pulled her through the shelves of shovels and rakes, to the back of the store where the indoors opened out again. That's where they kept the plants. Stepping into the green, they both breathed more deeply. Liam gave a little sigh.

"This is one of my favorite places," he said, beckoning her further into the leaves of it, stopping to look more closely at a fern, at a flower, at a sapling growing up from a plastic pot.

"You garden," she said, surprised that it surprised her, and then by how quickly it became a fundamental part of him in her mind. She could see, already, the way his hands would hold the plants, the gentle way that he would place them in the ground and pack the earth firm around them. He would talk to them too, she thought, give them small encouragements as they grew. She wondered if he ever sang to them. She'd read somewhere that singing helped plants grow.

"Just a little vegetable garden right now," he told her. "My housemates really love it. But I wanted to try some bulbs this year. I used to grow them back home. Daffodils. Tulips. Hyacinths. They're really pretty in the spring. But you have to plant them in fall so they have time to settle in."

The bulbs were displayed in a corner just inside the doors, jostling together in wooden bins.

"I used to think that babies came from bulbs," she told him as he sorted through the bins, choosing the small rooty things that would grow into flowers.

Liam smiled at her.

"I thought they turned into babies underground and then the infants had to claw their ways up to the surface."

"That's beautiful and terrifying," Liam told her.

"I was little. I think I must have mixed them up with sea turtles."

Liam held out his little bag of bulbs to her, proud of them already. "Alright. I think these are them."

On the bus ride back, he held her hand, the bag of bulbs nestled on the seat between them.

"I love the way you see things," he told her. "When I'm with you, it's like the world expands."

Jo wasn't sure exactly what he meant. She worried she'd unsettled him with her talk of bulbs and babies.

"Really," he said, responding to some subtle shift in her, as if he could sense her uncertainty. "Maybe you don't realize it. But you see the world so beautifully, with this kind of quiet magic. And, when I'm with you, I can almost see it too."

That night, as he slept beside her, she thought of the way he looked at those bulbs in the store, so full of love and wonder.

33

She stopped by Ness's once, in late September, when classes were beginning again. She wasn't sure what she would say. That she was dating someone else? That she missed her?

But Ness wasn't there to say anything to. One of her housemates answered the door and said she'd moved out weeks ago, come by to pick up her things, dropped out of school, gone off to Europe or New York or somewhere.

Jo couldn't move. She felt her feet rooting to the front steps, as if, in digging in, she could claw herself backwards. Ness had left. Ness was not coming back. It took her a moment to comprehend it fully. Ness had been back and left and never told her.

"You're Jo, right?" the housemate was asking.

Jo nodded.

"She left something for you. Just a second."

The housemate disappeared behind the door and Jo could hear footsteps on the stairs. She listened to the rhythmic sound of going up and coming down. One step at a time. No rush. Out on the porch, the light was slanting into autumn, the air just beginning to chill. The day was sunny with a cold breeze coming in.

The housemate returned with a rolled-up canvas. Jo knew which painting it would be. She took it, told the housemate "thank you," uprooted her feet, and walked away.

Back in her own room, she unrolled the painting. Something fell out of it, rolled under her bed. She had to reach to find it, feel around for it, pull it out from the shadowy space. A cone. Not a note. Not an explanation or apology or anything. Just a cone. It was small and compact, dense. It fit perfectly in the palm of her hand. She didn't know what type of tree it was from. Pine? Fir? Some other conifer? She didn't understand what Ness meant by it. She turned it over in her hand.

The cone seemed made of eyes, woody and half-closed. Between them, on the inside, the sparkle of sap. Jo peered in at it. As she turned the cone the glinting winked like embers. A pine-y scent came off it, the sharp of evergreen. For a moment, it was hot in her hand and alive. First, she put the cone on her desk, tried not to stare back at its eyes. Then, she put the cone in the desk drawer instead, hiding herself from its view.

She would not look up its name, would not try to determine what tree it came from. She would not try to solve the mystery of this message Ness had left her.

Soon, she would put the cone away in a box alongside her old notebooks from these months and only look at it when taken up by a wave of nostalgia. Years later, she will recognize the cone for what it is. Standing under the tree in the backyard of her new house, she will look down and see its matches blinking up at her. Sequoia.

But back then, Ness's painting laid out before her, she stood alone in her room staring back at herself.

The painting had not changed much since she'd stolen her first glimpse of it. Only the additions of a few more falling leaves, a few more lines of her verse filtering in.

Before she understood what she was doing, she'd grabbed a Sharpie from her desk. Uncapped it. Held it aloft above the paint. Its tip glinted, ready, but she did not know for what. She did not know what she could ever write to change this vision of herself looking back at her. She felt something nameless seeping out of her body, leaving her emptied, tired. It was over.

She put the Sharpie down. She rolled up the canvas and put it under her bed.

Afterward, she called Liam. She wouldn't tell him about the painting or the cone or the way Ness had disappeared. She would just ask him to lunch. She would just sit with him and talk about classes and drink a beer and let herself relax into the way he looked at her, his eyes all shining with something that she felt might become, might already be, love. She would lean into the warmth of him and be glad for how solid that warmth was, for how much his smile felt like a place that could be home.

He answered on the second ring.

34

All these years later, driving south through the valley to her old college town, Jo turns down a smaller highway through the forest and is met by a strand of burnt evergreens. The stillness, the silence of them, shocks her with an eerie sense of nothing. She wonders at that, realizes she can't feel anything, the way she usually can among trees. Even when that sense of them is hardly noticeable, it's an undercurrent, vaguely companionable, an almost curiosity, the sense of life meeting life.

Here, now, it is not there. The drive feels gruesome, this expanse of charred bodies, bark and wood burnt up branch to trunk to root. The jagged falls. The angles trees have come to rest at. In this moment, so close to the burning, it seems like there is nothing left alive.

The death of it all overwhelms her. Destruction impossibly vast. She knows she is only seeing a part of it. A sliver of the damage this one fire out of so many has wrought. A small swathe of land when around the state, the region, the world, there is so much death. From fire. From flood. From wind and avalanche. From smog and slow poison. She cannot comprehend it, the havoc of humans, the scale of the damage. The immensity of human guilt. The weight of human helplessness.

The earth is angry, she thinks. It has every right to be.

Behind the trees, the sunset glows red and orange, purple and blue, hot like the memory of flame. As the light shifts nightward, the trees become like shadows, dark against the darkening sky.

She wants to stop the car and pull over. She wants to get out and walk through the burnt trees. But she doesn't have the courage for that kind of witnessing. She knows if she touches the death in this landscape that closely, it will change her in ways she cannot comprehend. She does not stop. But she keeps looking, memorizing the shape of it, the way words won't find their ways out of the silence, as she drives through.

Coming off the highway, Jo turns down familiar streets that feel only half recognizable. It has been so long since she's had reason to come back here to her college town. There are new buildings where the old used to be, widened streets that used to be narrower, vacant lots that have turned into parking structures. Nearing campus, Jo drives past the park she used to go to, the café Ness used to work at, the bar she always went to with Liam. It is like no time has passed and all times have passed. She is dizzy with the dissonance of memory.

Her motel is across from the football stadium. She pulls into the parking lot and just sits for a minute, watching the sky darken to deeper blues. She feels a sense of unbeing, a mental mist she thinks that she should fight against. Instead, she lets it overtake her and, for a moment, she feels an almost nothingness. It is a kind of relief.

Her phone buzzes in the seat beside her. A text from Liam, an anxious checking in. She senses the pull of it, like a string that she is holding, a tether to lead her back.

She collects the phone and her keys, promising herself she will get some sleep tonight. She leaves the car to check in.

In the motel room, Jo unpacks her toiletries and brushes

her teeth and washes her face. For a moment, she thinks she needs to take a pill or an injection. She worries she hasn't packed the medications. Then, she remembers, she has stopped them. There are no pills or shots to take. An electric thrill runs through her whole body, a giddy irresponsible freedom. She is so light in it she thinks she will float away.

Jo calls Liam from the motel room.

She almost only texts to let him know she's arrived safely, to tell him where it is she has arrived to. But she needs to hear his voice. She thinks she hopes the sound of it will bring her back to herself, to her present life.

When he answers, he sounds worried.

"I'm here," she tells him.

"Where is here?" he asks. There is a hint of annoyance in the words.

"College," she says, keeping her tone light, giving him a little laugh.

"What?" he asks. "Why would you go there?"

She almost tells him about Ness, about the art show, thinks better of it.

"Nostalgia?" she says, trying to put the sound of a self-effacing shrug in her voice. "It's a place to be, I guess."

"Huh," Liam says. "I guess I thought you were going somewhere more relaxing. You said the coast."

"I thought about it," she lies. "Here just seemed familiar."

He doesn't say anything. That worries her.

"Are you angry at me?" she asks him.

She knows she is pushing. She isn't sure why, what exactly she wants him to say to her. She wants, she thinks, to push past the distance, to be on the other side of it, to get to that place they find where they begin to comprehend each other.

"I'm just—I worry when you get like this."

His voice is strained, the strung-too-tight sound it gets when he is trying to hold something back. She wishes he would simply shout his anger at her so they could move on.

"Get like what?" she asks.

Liam sighs. "Erratic. What would happen if we had a child, and you did this? Just ran off like this?"

The words circle inside her, buzzing. *Erratic. Child. Ran off.* She would never leave a child. They do not have a child. Now she is angry.

"I didn't just run off," she snaps. "If I were truly erratic. If I ever did run off, you wouldn't know. I wouldn't tell you. I wouldn't call. You'd just have to figure it out yourself."

She hears his intake of breath through the phone, sharp. She wishes she could see his face, could know what he is thinking.

There is a long pause. She almost says they shouldn't do this on the phone. She almost says let's talk when I get back. She almost apologizes. But he speaks first.

"There's something wrong with you," he tells her. There is a blankness in his voice when he says it, like a part of him is no longer reachable. "It isn't just the IVF. You can't just blame the hormones. It's always been there. And now you run away when we're so close to what you said you wanted? I thought you wanted a family with me? It makes no sense. You make no sense."

She knows, later, she will cry over this. Later, she will feel the despair that sets in when she runs up against the knowledge that her husband does not fully understand her, may never fully comprehend her, that part of her is a stranger to him, still, after so many years, that part of her is still a stranger to herself. Later, she will feel the loneliness of that. But now, she feels an eerie calm come over her.

"Just because I don't make *your* sense doesn't mean I don't make sense."

He doesn't say anything. She waits. Still hoping he might. Still hoping that blankness will go out of his voice and the sound of his care will return. But she hears nothing.

"I'm going to go now," she says. "We should both get some sleep."

She waits again, hoping he might say he loves her before he hangs up. Then she will say it back. And they will not be fighting anymore.

"Okay," he says. "Good night then."

He hangs up first.

35

In the morning, Jo walks by the river where she used to write poetry. She has a notebook in her bag just in case. She is fairly certain, however, that no words will come. Her mind drifts, still thinking of her call with Liam the night before, still wondering if she should text an apology. She is worrying over her plans to meet Ness, how Ness has said she will arrive in town tomorrow, that she will call her when she gets in. She checks her phone nervously, still a day too early. What if, now she's here, Ness will not call, will not come, will simply vanish? What if she will be left here all alone, caught between times? At dawn, she was surprised to wake up in the motel and not in one of her old college bedrooms. She keeps thinking, as she walks, that she is late for class.

The day is cool and cloudy, threatening rain. Few people pass her. There is an almost solitude in the sounds of the wind through the leaves and the water. The memory of this place, this town and this path by its river, feels distant, like a haze overlaid on the day. She cannot quite place herself in it. She feels the years lining up between eras of her life, a veil of time, how it has altered her.

The river path is the same as it was but now, she thinks, she can see it more clearly. Now, she knows the names of the trees. In her years of true adulthood, she has learned them. She has bought the guidebooks and the plant apps and set herself the task of pursuing an arboreal language. Now, looking, she can see the different kinds of firs and maples. She knows the words for them, the vine maples, the bigleaf maples, the cedars and the hemlock and the Douglas firs. She even notices, can even sometimes name, the mushrooms sprouting up from under newly fallen leaves.

She sees now, though she never did before, a path below the path, a narrow deer trail, winding beneath the underbrush. She ducks through a tangle of branches and finds herself in a space she did not know existed. Below the main path and above the river, a fallen tree, mossy and crumbling with age, and a kind of clearing, just large enough for a person to pace in. Three vine maples reach their roots down to the river below, exposed, their surrounding dirt worn away. She can hear the water rushing, though she cannot see it.

This, she thinks, is a hidden place, a place set apart. World between worlds. She is certain it cannot be seen from the main path above, shielded as it is by the branches of trees and the tangles of sloping undergrowth. She wonders how many have found it, if students meet here by moonlight. There are no empty beer cans or wrappers or cigarettes, none of the human traces she would expect to find in such a place.

There is a shift in the air, subtly startling, like a breeze that grows incrementally warmer as it touches the skin. There is a rustling, strong as the sound feathers make as they rush past an ear. The river grows louder and the rhythm of its currents pulses through her toes.

A laugh burbles up beside her and she turns.

"Oh! Sorry, I didn't know—"

The laugh is familiar, the voice, the face, the sense of her there beside her.

"Jo?"

"Ness."

Jo feels the pull toward and away in equal force. It traps her in place. Through the echoing tumble of water, years pass between them. They both are and are not who they were, are, will be.

It's Ness who speaks first, breaks through the sound of the river below with a "Hi."

"Hi," Jo repeats.

"It's strange," Ness says, "I was just walking and here was this little trail. I've never seen this place before, but it must have been here. I just never noticed."

Ness has launched right into conversation, and it takes Jo a beat to catch up, to understand Ness's words and the meaning of them, to understand that words have any meaning at all.

"Neither did I," Jo says. "I came to the river all the time to write, though. Even after—"

"That spring," Ness finishes for her. Jo wishes she could read her voice better, could understand whether the tones are full of longing or amusement or regret.

"Yeah," Jo says.

Just a spring. She is surprised to realize it was only a season, that time that seems essential, every moment a piece in the foundation that underpins her sense of her self.

"I didn't know you'd gotten in already. I thought tomorrow, that you'd call when you arrived," Jo says. "I would have called you if I'd known."

Ness shrugs. "I changed my train. They needed me for a talk today."

"Oh."

Ness is staring at her now with a look that seems like curiosity.

"It's good to see you," she says. "You look exactly the same."

36

They walk to the café where Ness used to work and order two coffees.

"Wow," Ness says when they step inside. "They've redone it."

It looks much the same from the outside, but, past the front doors, they have stepped into a space that is completely unfamiliar. It takes Jo a moment to orient herself, to realize that a wall has been knocked down to make a wider open space for seating, that that's why it is as if the inside of the café has grown. The ugly old linoleum flooring and peeling wallpaper have been replaced by clean lines of wood paneling. The light fixtures look old in the trendy, understated kind of way that means they are quite new.

"It's nice," Jo says.

Ness sighs. "I know. I wish they'd turned it all white and chrome and minimalist so I could hate it like a good old curmudgeon."

Jo laughs. "You're not old."

Ness drops her bag onto the table and sinks dramatically into her chair. "I'm forty. I'm practically dead."

Jo shakes her head.

"Oh, you'll get it soon enough. You've got, what, two, three years left?"

"One."

"Well. Better pop out that baby soon. You know what they

say about pregnancy over forty."

Jo is surprised by the words. She doesn't remember Ness being this blunt, skirting this unthinkingly close to cruelty.

"Thirty-five is geriatric," Jo tells her.

"What?"

"It's officially called a geriatric pregnancy at that age. You're considered higher risk. You get slated for all the extra tests."

"That's wild."

"It is."

"Who has babies before thirty-five on purpose anymore?"

"Lots of people do."

"Hm."

They sip their coffees and enter into a pause that lengthens into a quiet that begins to frighten Jo. She isn't sure what lies inside it. It feels full and fraught, a place that could sink them both. In that quiet, Jo cannot bring herself to look at Ness directly.

"So, an art show?" Jo says, attempting to dissipate whatever this silence is building between them.

Ness waves her hand as if to bat it away. "Oh, they just needed a graduate who was still making art. We get rarer by the year. Like some kind of endangered species. They all go into branding now."

"I went into branding."

Ness raises an eyebrow, then frowns. "Well, sure, but not really."

"Not really?"

"I mean, it's just your day job. You still write poetry, don't you?"

Jo shrugs. "Not like I used to. Not like I thought I would."

"Why not?"

"I don't know. The words are just…not quite there any-more. They warp into slogans or they're just…inert."

Ness doesn't say anything, simply waits, and Jo finds her-self continuing, confiding like she used to. "It didn't use to feel like that. It used to feel like, sometimes, I could string them together, if they were just the right ones, and they'd almost be like something more than words, like a force, like they were writing themselves, like a spell or something…"

Jo let's herself trail off. She can't read the look Ness is giving her, can't tell whether it is pity or disappointment or embar-rassment. She feels suddenly wretched. She wishes she hadn't said anything, can't understand why she did. It horrifies her, how vulnerable she has made herself with this person she hardly knows anymore, who she hasn't really spoken to in years. She thinks of all the other hopefuls in the fertility clin-ic, raw with their baby longing, offering their arms for the blood draws, their veins for the shots, their insides for the harvesting. She was terrified, each and every visit, at how much was revealed of her. By the end of a pregnancy, if she could even have a pregnancy, she felt certain she'd be per-manently wearing her skin inside-out.

She worries now, mortified, as she heaves her deepest fears onto the table between them for Ness's inspection, that she already might be.

"You know," Ness says, "after college, I didn't paint for years."

"Really?"

"I just lost the sense of it for a while. It came back, though, eventually. It always comes back. You can't really stop being an artist. It's your nature."

37

As the morning wears on, while Ness goes to give her talk and help set up the art show, Jo wanders the campus, visiting memories: the library where she used to read for hours, enchanted by the vast worlds it held rustling through all those pages; the student union where she spent every finals week sustaining herself on bagels and class notes; the steps of the English building where she learned to talk about poetry outside the bounds of a classroom. And, here, her old hiding spot. She'd loved so many trees on campus, but this was the one she would come to when she wanted to be invisible. The tree rises up on the outskirts of the quad, tall and evergreen, branches draping all the way to the ground around the trunk that is far too thick to wrap one's arms around. She recognizes the tree when she sees them now, knows the name she didn't know before. Sequoia. She ducks underneath. There is a branch that runs along the ground and arches up to make an almost seat. She remembers the first time she brought Liam here, how it felt like sharing a secret, like inviting him into a part of herself that was hidden.

"Wow," he'd said, circling the tree's vast trunk. "It's incredible. It must be so old."

"They're beautiful, aren't they?" Jo said and watched Liam frown at her avoidance of *it*, confused for a moment, before realizing she meant the tree.

"Yeah," he said, smiling, and pulling her in for a kiss.

Now, she takes a picture of the tree and texts him. *At our old spot.*

On the ground, all the cones stare up at her, blinking.

38

Back at the motel, her phone buzzes with a text from Liam. *Sorry to be so snappish last night. I'm just worried. Hope you're ok.*

She texts back right away. *I'm sorry too. Call you tonight? Love you.*

She waits for him to respond, then sets the phone on the nightstand while she gathers up the painting to bring to Ness. She unrolls it, lays it out on the bed. She has not looked at it in years. Now, she is surprised by its beauty. In her mind, it was always ugly, terrifying, a picture of a woman subsumed and disappearing. But now, it seems different. The woman's face, Jo's face, made of wood, merging into tree. The poems scrolling up and down, becoming bark, leaf, sunlight. It seems less like disappearance now. It seems like something else entirely.

womantree, leafpoem, wordlight

It is a kind of interweaving, all the elements so close they can't be pulled apart. They move into each other. They change each other's shape.

Liam's text now. *Love you too.*

And then Ness, directly after, texts as well. *At the gallery. Meet at the gift shop when you're ready?*

She remembers the sequoia cone that fell from the canvas that first time she unrolled it, the way it glistened on the inside, hidden, sealed.

Jo rolls up the painting, but her hands are reluctant. She wants to look longer. She wants to stay a few more moments in this one, this moment when she sees it, what she thinks Ness meant, what she thinks Ness saw in her, back then, this magic.

39

Jo walks through the quad with the painting rolled up and tucked under her arms. She walks past the sequoia. She passes under the tall Douglas firs that line the walk to the art museum, remembers the shade of them on hot days, the way the sun cast about in their branches.

She enters the museum through the gift shop, the only part of the place that doesn't require a fee. Back in college, she worked the register for a season, selling art books and postcards and prints to alumni and visiting parents. Students never came into the shop. It was not priced for them. Even the postcards were expensive.

This afternoon, a student reads a book behind the register while Ness looks over a table of seashells. The shells are painted in bright colors and glinting with a gold finish. Ness's head is tilted to the side as she picks the shells up and puts them down again. Her lips are pursed as she examines them. Her eyes are sharp and critical. Jo wants to watch her longer, but Ness looks up, sensing her there, and smiles.

"Come look at these."

Up close, the shells shine even brighter, brilliant greens and blues and purples. Inside, they hold intricate paintings of mermaids or seahorses or crabs.

"What do you think?" Ness asks her.

"They're pretty," Jo says, cautiously, knowing Ness is about to share an opinion of them, not wanting to be caught on the wrong side of it.

"Sure," Ness says, "beautiful even. But why shells? I mean, if you're going to paint all the way over them like this in such un-shell colors and then paint your picture in the center with so little regard for the form of the shell itself, I mean, why couldn't they just paint on a ceramic circle or something. It's a waste of a good shell."

"How would you do it?"

Ness smiles, her eyes sparking up with ideas. "I'd work with the shells. I'd let them tell me what to paint and how. I'd let their colors come through. Use a more translucent paint. Maybe watercolor. I'd let their shapes guide the lines."

She laughs at herself. "I'm sorry. Look at me. All passionate about painting shells."

"It's fine," Jo says, "It's nice. I'd like to see your version. They sound perfect."

Ness shrugs. "Most of this kind of thing is just tourist junk. I don't know. Maybe though, it could be something."

Ness's gaze goes distant, and Jo knows she is thinking, an idea, a new creation. She can almost see the vision of it vibrating in the air around Ness like some elemental force. And, for a moment, Jo experiences a deep, painful envy.

The moment moves and Ness has taken her hand.

"Come," she says. "They've almost finished setting up the paintings."

The student art gallery is the smallest, set off in a corner of the building with one wall reserved for visiting alumni artists. She feels Ness's paintings before she sees them. A current that catches her up. She has to move toward them. They are deep swirls of green and blue shot through with orange and gold.

They find form in a kind of shapelessness. There is strange-ness in the brush strokes, as if they are trying to emerge, as if they have been caught and held mid-creation. They remind Jo of looking at clouds when the winds are high, the way the sky shifts so quickly so that the moment a shape begins to come clear, it changes.

"What do you think?" Ness asks and Jo hears an edge of nerves in her voice.

"They're beautiful. It's like you've caught the paint midwave."

Ness smiles. "Midwave. I like that."

They stare at the paintings for another moment, letting the colors wash over them. Jo thinks she must be visibly glowing with it, whatever it is Ness has brought into being here, in this tiny corner of this tiny room with these paintings that seem so vast in their seeming simplicity.

"You brought it," Ness says, finally, gesturing to the canvas that Jo has forgotten in her arms, still rolled up.

"Right. Yes."

Fingertips brush as she hands over the painting. Skin sparks off skin. They move through it, smile in grown up embarrassment. But there is a moment before they collect themselves, almost imperceptible, where the meeting of eyes makes a current in the air there between them, and, below that, the roots twining under.

"I can't believe you kept it," Ness is saying. Her laugh is forced and light, a little too breathy.

"Why wouldn't I?"

Ness shrugs. "I don't know. I always kind of thought you hated it."

Ness rolls the painting out on the floor, and now, they are kneeling beside it, catching the details. Jo expects it to seem out of place here, amidst Ness's newer work, her newer style. But, somehow, it doesn't. There is the similarity of a thing frozen in the midst of a movement, paused right at the moment of change.

"You didn't mark it," Ness says.

"What?" Jo asks. She can't have understood. Ness can't mean what she fears she might. Her heart turns to a winged creature caught in her chest.

"Like the others," Ness says. "I was so sure you'd have marked this one too. But you haven't, have you?"

"You knew?"

Ness laughs again, a laugh of true amusement. "Of course I did. You thought I didn't?"

Jo knows her cheeks are pinkening, hot and guilty.

"I always looked forward to seeing what you'd put in them. You were subtle, but so…I don't know. It was so gutsy. I loved it."

"It was petty."

Ness shrugs. "Sure. But gutsy petty."

40

The next evening, on her way to Ness's show, the river path catches Jo's feet. It pulls her past the lamplights to the trail that runs beneath.

Few walkers are out as she ducks through the undergrowth to follow the narrow deer trail. The light is dim amidst the leaves and, as she walks, it is as if she is tunneling into the heart of the forest. When she hears the hum of the river below and a laugh drifting down from the main path above, she is surprised to remember she is not alone with the trees but poised in a still space between the flow of people and water.

She comes to the fallen mossy trunk, to the vine maples that grow up around it. The fallen tree makes a seat, and she takes it, leans her back against one of the maples, looks up at their greengold leaves. The air holds the foreknowledge of rain about to break through.

The tree is warm where she leans up against it. A subtle heat radiates from the bark. She thinks of the sequoia in her backyard in the early morning the week before—only the week before—the way she felt the heat of the tree brushing her hand. Beneath her, the roots of the three maples roam underground. They are reaching toward her.

She knows it is impossible.

She closes her eyes and leans into that impossibility, lets its warmth wrap around her. In the rush of the river and the

patter of rain, she begins to hear words
    rootfeet
    murmur in the underground
    trunkbelly up
    branchrise through the leafhair
    tangle in the skymind
    wind round the windwhisper
    wavepulse steadyhot
    thrum
There is a poem in her but to move is to break the spell. She reaches for her phone, types it fast with clumsy thumbs, catches less than half of it, her mind still caught in treewindwaterground.

Her thumbs slip on water on screen, and she notices the downpour, the way the clouds have crowded in above. Her hair is already dripping with wet. The rush of the river moves onward. The trees are distant now, their attention gone elsewhere as the rain patters through their leaves.

42

At the gallery, the poems rustle in her phone in her bag and the drip of the damp in her hair. She is late. She has lost track of time. The professors and students and parents and visiting artists mingle awkwardly with pastries and coffee for the student exhibition. When Ness sees Jo, she pulls her outside.

The rain has paused, and the light of the day is just beginning to fade, the clouds tinting pink.

"I need to run an errand," she says. "Do you want to come? I could use a ride."

"Don't they need you in there?" Jo asks.

They have wandered out to the quad where groups of students are just beginning to emerge for their evenings, walking in groups to the dining hall, wandering off to the bars and restaurants and cafés that surround the campus. There's a sense of relaxed celebration about them. It's only the third week of term. The year is still just beginning.

Ness shrugs. "Not really. I made an appearance."

Her eyes are shining in a way Jo hasn't seen before. Something is buzzing inside her, a mystery that Jo cannot name.

"Where are you going?" she asks.

Ness smiles, knowing she will come. "On an adventure."

They take Jo's car, driving south out of town, following the bends of the river as it moves through housing developments and then further out into forest. They drive in near silence, Ness occasionally calling the turns from the map on her phone. Jo still does not know where they are going, what they are going for. "To pick something up from a friend of a friend" is all Ness has told her. Jo's practical self thinks she should insist on more clarity, but another self, the self that gets the car and drives it, the self that follows Ness's directions, doesn't care, is simply content to be driving through the darkening twilight with Ness in the passenger seat beside her.

They pull off the main highway and onto a series of streets that narrow, finally, to a dirt road winding into the trees. The shadows of leaves crowd around them as Jo listens to the crunch of the wheels.

"This must be it," Ness says, pointing to a light that glows ahead of them. As they drive closer, the structure comes clear: the porchlight and the light from the downstairs window illuminating the old farmhouse with its mossy roof and westward lean.

Jo stops the car, pulls the key from the ignition. Without the headlights, they are enveloped in the dusk.

She turns to Ness. "Okay. I think you should probably tell me what we're doing now."

Ness shakes her head. "You won't believe me."

"Try."

"Looking for a selkie skin," Ness says. That buzz around her is growing and there is excitement in her eyes.

"A what?"

"Just come with me."

Ness doesn't give Jo a chance to respond. She opens the passenger door and steps out. Jo follows. They climb the porch steps that creak alarmingly under their feet. Ness knocks on the door. Jo hears footsteps on the floorboards inside. A woman answers, long gray hair catching the lights of the house in a diffusing glow.

"You must be Ness," the woman says.

Ness nods. "And this is my friend Jo."

"Come in."

The woman leads them into a living room that is filled with glass mushrooms. They cover every flat surface, from bookshelves to end tables. The light glints off them, creating an impression of glisten and glitter. It is like stepping into a space of strange magic.

"Wow," Ness says. "Do you make them?"

The woman nods.

"They're incredible."

"Thank you. They're fascinating, aren't they?"

"Mushrooms?"

"Fungi. You know mushrooms are only the visible parts, the fruit. The fungi themselves are so much larger. All their little threads beneath what we can see."

Jo imagines the fungi as the woman describe them, the silver tendrils running underground, reaching out for each other.

"You kind of capture that," Ness says, bending to look a row of mushrooms straight on, "in the way the colors thread inside the glass."

The woman smiles. "You're an artist too."

"I paint. Ocean mostly, these days."

"Of course. You have that sense of water about you. My sister had it too. Let me get the box."

The woman leaves them in the living room with the mushrooms and the light. They hear her footsteps on the stairs.

"This is…interesting," Jo says, when the woman's steps have faded.

"It's fine," Ness tells her. "She's a girlfriend's partner's friend from college. I never go into stranger's houses without some kind of connection. Not anymore anyway. I learned that early on."

"You do this a lot?" Jo asks. "Going into strangers' houses to look for…selkie skins?"

Ness laughs. There is an edge to the laugh, a discomfort. "You make it sound so silly when you say it like that."

Jo tries to think of a way to reassure her, but the glint of the glass mushrooms, the night darkening outside the window, the strangeness of the house and the woman and this quest Ness seems to be on, envelop her and take her words. She doesn't know what she should say.

Ness is still looking at all the glass mushrooms, examining them one by one without touching them.

"It's really amazing," she is saying, "how many artists live around here. You'd never know how much incredible work is being done in peoples' houses and sheds and garages."

The woman returns with an old cardboard box. Ness leans forward as she opens it, gently unfolding the lid, and brings out a dusty fur.

"According to family legend," the woman says, "It was my great-great-great-grandmother's. She kept it hidden all her life so the family wouldn't know what she really was. Then, on her deathbed, she told my great-great-grandmother where she'd hidden it under the attic floorboards. And we've passed it on through the family ever since. Her selkie skin."

Ness reaches a hand out to touch it, cautious and gentle, but already, Jo can tell, disappointed. The buzzing has left her.

"It's just an old fur," she says quietly.

"Of course," the woman says. "What else would an old selkie skin be?"

Ness shakes her head.

"You don't believe the story?" the woman asks.

"I'm sorry. It just—I don't think it's what I'm looking for."

"How do you know what you're looking for if you've never seen it?"

"I've seen a lot of old furs."

"Your friend told me. You've been looking a long time. Travelling. All over the country, she told me. Even the world."

Ness nods.

"How many have you seen? There must be a lot of old family stories like this. There must be so many old boxes filled with so many old skins."

"I've lost count."

The woman nods.

"What if what you've been looking for is exactly what you've been looking at? Maybe you just need to look deeper."

"I'm sorry for wasting your time," Ness tells her.

"No time wasted. It was nice to meet you both."

The woman folds the fur back into the box and leads them to the door. She stops at the entryway table, picks up one of the glass mushrooms glowing there. She looks at it, then hands it to Ness.

"I think this one belongs to you," she says. "A gift."

Ness tries to hand it back. "I couldn't—"

The woman pushes it into her hands again. "It's already yours."

Back in the car, Ness looks at the glass in her hands. The stem of the mushroom is awhirl with greenblue threads. In its cap, held right at the center, a seed.

"That's a real maple seed," Jo says, looking at the way the threads from the stem rise up to curl around it.

"It's so intricate," Ness says. "It must have been hard to make."

"This isn't why you quit college, is it?" Jo asks abruptly. "To look for—"

Ness shakes her head. "Let's drive back. I don't want to sit in her driveway too long."

Jo turns the key in the ignition, steers the car around to drive back to the road.

"They're always artists," Ness is murmuring, and Jo can't tell if she is talking to her or to herself. "They always make these incredible things."

They are back on the highway when the rain begins, blurring the lights of the cars that drive around them.

"I never told you what happened, did I?" Ness asks. "Why I left in college?"

"No," Jo says, keeping her eyes on the road. "You never did."

Ness sighs and looks out the window, watching the rain, still holding the mushroom.

"My grandma died. You know, the one with the selkie stories. After you and I went to the coast. While my parents and I were sorting out the house and the water damage. We got this call. The staff at the retirement home said she just walked out into the Sound one night before they realized what was happening. She sunk underwater. She didn't come up."

"Oh. Ness. I'm so sorry."

Ness shakes her head. "I didn't know what to tell you. I mean, it sounds so silly: *My grandma died so I quit college and never talked to my girlfriend again.* But…we were having all those dreams and then, the night before my parents and I got the call, I dreamed my grandma found a selkie skin and put it on and then it was all just light and water."

The night pulls close around them. The rain. The head-lights glinting off the pavement and the water-soaked air.

"I wish I'd known," Jo says. "I would have tried harder to find you."

"No. I was a pretty strange person for a few years after that."

"You're always a pretty strange person." She keeps her voice gentle when she says it, tries to bring a light mischief to it, so Ness knows she is teasing.

Ness laughs. "But it wasn't in a good way for a while."

"So that's when you started looking for them?"

"Yeah," Ness says. "I don't know what I hope to find. I think maybe I just want to see one, to feel it, to know if it's true or not."

"How would you know?"

Ness shakes her head. "I have no idea. I just think I would feel something…familiar."

They've come into town. Jo winds them through neighbor-hoods, taking the long way.

"Where are you staying?" she asks. "I'll drop you there."

Ness shakes her head. "Just drive back to your motel. I want to walk."

They walk together, back to the dark campus, tracing the paths under the trees, neither wanting to leave the other just yet. The rain has slowed to a drizzle, almost just a mist. They reach the edge of the quad and come to Jo's old tree.

"Come on," she says, pulling Ness under the branches. "I'm showing you my secret spot."

She does it now, she thinks, to cheer Ness up, to show her something beautiful. But she wonders why she never showed her then, back in college, this spot of hers. She showed Liam but not Ness. Maybe it was because they were always going to

Ness's special places. By comparison, her own never seemed special enough to share.

"I used to come here all the time," Jo says, "to read. Or just to sit."

"I know."

"How?"

"I saw you sitting here all the time when I was walking to class."

"Why didn't you ever say hi?"

"I didn't want to bother you. It was your secret spot. You came here when you wanted to be alone, right? I didn't want to intrude."

"Oh."

Beneath the tree's branches, it is dark and hard to see. The glow of the campus paths seems far away.

"I came here right before I left town, though. Did you get the cone I wrapped in the painting?" Ness asks.

"Yes."

Ness smiles. "It's from here. I was sitting right under this tree, trying to write you a note, trying to tell you what happened before I left and then a cone dropped down right next to me. And I knew it was for you. It was like the tree had a message for you or something."

Jo thinks of the cone, the way it stared at her. She can't remember what happened to it. She wishes she could see it again, find whatever it might have been trying to tell her.

"You never sent the note," she tells Ness.

"I think I hoped the cone and the painting would somehow tell you everything."

"They didn't."

The kiss overtakes her before she knows it is happening.

back to bark

and evergreen
nightshadow filter
scenting of needles
crunch the underfoot
          caught
                    in the circle
                      of rootbranch.

Jo puts her hands between them, pushes back.

"I have a husband now," she says as if the presence of a husband could break the spell of the wave that engulfs her.

"Does it matter?"

"Yes."

Ness blinks at her as if waking. "Right," she says. "Of course. I'm sorry."

They are in the in-between now, in and out of the past, in and out of the world. They stay there a moment, letting uncertainty circle them.

"I should go," Ness says.

"I should probably go back to the motel. Make some phone calls."

"Coffee in the morning?" Ness asks. There is an edge of worry in her tone, as if she thinks Jo will refuse.

"That'd be nice."

43

Later that night, a text from Liam.

Good time to call?

She is not sleeping. She is thinking of Ness, of the kiss, of the mushrooms and the search for selkie skins. She is reading the fragments of the poem she caught earlier that evening. She is trying to find the roots that run between them.

She texts back. *About to sleep. Tomorrow?*

Ok. Sleep well. Love you.

Love you.

44

That night, the dream:

seed float in
        a circle of rain
silver threaded shoot
        unfurled to breaking
bit by bit
        sprout glint
curl in curl out
        the sun is dreaming
underground wait
        for the move of the moon

45

When she and Ness meet for coffee the next morning, they don't talk about the night before, the glass mushrooms, the selkie skin, the story, the kiss. Instead, Ness shows her a sketch.

"I woke up in the middle of the night from a dream and just painted it," Ness says.

It is Jo's dream. Seed. Threads. Water. The floating and unfurling. The rays of the sun peeking in at the corners.

Jo reaches for her notebook, turns to the page of the poem she scribbled in the earliest parts of the morning, hands it across the table, watches Ness's face while she reads, the way the smile curls upward, brightening.

When Ness finishes the poem, she darts her eyes up to Jo's, astonished. They can't find the words for the wonder that floats there between them, so they laugh.

46

It is familiar, but different, the way the dreams come, making poems and paintings. They know better, now, what they must do with it.

Ness is using the university studio space reserved for visiting artists, a small room on the fourth floor of the arts building. Two days after the first dream, three more dreams later, Ness brings Jo there. The windows look out on a grove of old firs.

"They built around them," Ness says when she sees Jo gazing at the greenblue of their branches. "Isn't that amazing? They could have cut them down and made it simpler, cheaper, but they didn't. I've always loved that about this building."

Jo spreads her poems out on the table. She isn't sure what she will find when she looks at them. They've come in the middle of the night or while walking. They've come in lines and fragments. She can't tell how they piece together.

Ness lays out her sketches. Some watercolors. Rough outlines of the visions she's trying to capture.

They stare down at their papers. Ness rubs her forehead, leaving a shadow of pencil lingering there from her hand.

"Right," she says. "Okay."

Jo can see her thinking, the way the ideas are parsing out behind her eyes. She shakes her head, puts a hand on Ness's elbow.

"Not yet."

Jo can feel the way the poems and the pictures connect, the little warm threads that move between them. They make a web. She can't see it, exactly, but she knows it is there. She moves their papers around the table, pairing, grouping, arranging. Ness begins to see it too. They move them together. Then they look at what they've done.

Seed held in water shifts to tiny creature floating silver-furred shifts to cone alight with fire shifts to ball of silver tendrils reaching outward into dark.

"It's the same thing," Ness says, "over and over again in different images."

"What thing?"

"A potential."

47

Ness's paint meanders. Jo's words spiral in over themselves. Nothing seems right when they try to bring them together in the ways that they did before: the writing over or under the paint, the painting of words into pictures. The words are too long or too short to fit the images, the paint doesn't hold them. Some connection between them is missing.

It is Jo's idea to bring in the trees. She is gazing out the window at the firs, pondering what words she might use to catch the tenor of their branches brushing through the wind, when she begins to wonder what they would do in the paint.

"Hm," Ness says when Jo suggests it, glancing up from her canvas with a look of defeat. "Why not? Couldn't be worse than this."

Outside, the air is still damp with morning mist. They collect the fallen twigs beneath the trees. Jo picks up a few cones as well and some yellowgreen leaves that have just begun to drift from the maples. On their way back into the building, Ness pulls a sprig of lavender and collects some drooping rose petals. Back in the studio, they spread their treasure out on the table to dry.

Ness starts to use the fir twigs immediately, dipping them into her paint and letting the needles feather out over the canvas.

She steps back to look, "Huh. Maybe."

Jo spends the rest of the morning writing her poems out on the leaves and petals. Ness begins to glue them onto her canvases, creating a collage affect, building up layer over layer.

"We'll use a good sealant," Ness says, "when we're done. That should keep them."

Jo thinks of the way the leaves and petals will decay over time, the color seeping out of them while the paint stays vibrant, and the ink of the words grows bolder in the fade. She thinks it will be beautiful.

48

They work in the studio and walk by the river to collect their leaves and petals and needles. They stop, sometimes, for lunch or coffee. Ness darts away for two afternoons to give talks to the art students. Jo texts Liam pictures of the places they used to go when they dated and leaves him three reassuring voicemails. Otherwise, their time is their own.

They begin to paint and write the eclipse before it comes. Jo tells herself it is just the atmosphere of it, the excitement they are catching as everyone buzzes about the totality that hasn't been seen here, in this place, for almost half a century. But there is something about the way she and Ness render it that echoes the other images. Moon inside sun. Sun inside moon. Moon crescent shadows held at the centers of leaves. They are reaching toward something. Or something is reaching toward them.

49

Miss you, Liam texts.
Miss you too.
How are things?
Fine. Writing again.
That's great! Sounds like a vacation is just what you needed.
Guess so ☺
Home soon?
Home soon.

50

Leafshadow made of moons. Crescents on the ground, the fluttering lightdark shift of them. Jo holds out her hand to watch them dance across her skin, palming a celestial shade.

This morning, both the quiet and the buzz. People crowd the sidewalks, seeking space to watch from. Jo and Ness have traced the river path, today, filled with fellow walkers out to see the eclipse. They've come to a field full of lawn chairs and picnic blankets. They sit by a small grove of trees a little way off from the crowds. They have their special glasses like the rest, goofy and square. Ness takes a picture of Jo in hers.

"You look like a vision of the future the past had," she says. "Like you should have a jetpack and a flying car or something."

Jo laughs, takes the glasses off and folds their flimsy cardboard temples inward toward the rims. "At least we won't damage our eyes."

"Yeah," Ness says, twirling her own glasses between her fingers, "You'd think they would have updated these things since the 60s, though. Do all those serious eclipse chasers wear these? They seem so…amateur."

"They probably have better ones."

The morning is festive and expectant. They watch families with children running up the path. They watch college students lounging in the sun. The day is clear. They all feared the clouds, but the clouds did not show. They have the perfect view of the sun and moon approaching each other, steady and incremental.

Earlier that morning, in the motel before meeting Ness, Jo missed a call from Liam. She almost called back, almost listened to the voicemail, decided against it because she was already running late. She'd listen later, she thought. She'd call after.

Here, now, across the field, the watchers grow restless. The sky is slow, dimming bit by bit. Birds fly over them, into the trees. Frogs croak in the grass. Crickets chirp their lullabies. The air turns cold.

The hush descends as the birds move from nightsong to silence. The frogs and crickets quiet. The world falls dark. The people around them seem to fall away. Through her glasses, she sees the sun and moon embrace. She reaches for Ness's hand and finds Ness already reaching for her.

When the sun and moon reach their totality, she pulls her glasses off. That is the sight she will always remember. The softsharpcold of it. The white of the light that they make. The way it glows like love, strange and inhuman. Uncanny, the deep of the shadow. A beautiful terror. She knows she is seeing apocalypse, and it is nothing like she imagined. The world ends in a slow rush of wonder.

51

It is like coming back from the dead. The earth warms again. The hush lifts. But they are still muted, startled out of themselves and into something else they cannot fully comprehend. Jo experiences an intense desire for sugar and caffeine.

They are still holding hands as they follow the river path back toward campus and their café. Jo does not notice the holding at first and, by the time she does, it feels too late to pull her hand away. She doesn't really want to. There is something right in it, the warmcold of their fingers interlocking.

When they pass the head of the deer trail, they both turn to follow it. Jo cannot tell who is leading who. They come to the mossy trunk, the vine maples that rise up around it. Jo is sure the trees are watching her, in some way aware of her presence.

They see, then, what they hadn't seen before, not on the morning they met here, not when Jo came back for the poem: another trail, even narrower, continues downward. They step over the fallen tree, move under the eyes of the vine maples, and follow it. It is almost impassable for the brambles that grow up around it. Ness goes ahead, still holding Jo's hand. It is damp and mud squelches around their shoes. At one point, it becomes so narrow, they almost have to turn back but, pushing through, they find the place where the trail opens up again: a little clearing beneath a big leaf maple, just large enough to fit the broad roots as they curve up around themselves and reach down toward the river. The river is visible now, flowing steadily beneath them. It is louder here, the sound of the current.

"We're almost right on top of the water," Ness whispers.

Jo's eyes are caught in the shadows flitting over the ground, all those half-moons rising up from fallen golden leaves. The sun still holds the memory of the moon even as the two bodies move onward to opposite points of the sky. On the tree and around it, the leaves all eerie autumn yellow, reflecting light and water. She picks up a fallen leaf. It is startlingly large, wider than the hand she holds it with. Grasping it, she is sure that the tree has called them here, that, when they came here before, the path to this place had been hidden, secret, but now, in this in-between moment of sun meeting moon, day meeting night, it has appeared for them.

Ness is looking out over the river, eyes shining with the blue. Above her, the maple glows golden, spreading wide. A cool breeze rustles through.

Jo pulls Ness toward her. In this space outside the world, in this time between times, she is deliberate. Her hands on Ness's cheek, in her hair, lengthening the seconds between them. She thinks of the sunmoon kiss when their lips touch, the cold of the glowing embrace that ends worlds, begins new ones.

Now, there is nowhere but here, her hands on the soft of Ness's skin, moving under the warmth of her shirt, Ness's fingers undoing buttons, slipping down.

Their bodies move together, against, around, into each other under the skyshift of gold and blue. Glancing over her, over Ness, over all of them, the sunmoonshadows, multiplying. They all tangle up with the roots that grow around them, with the water that runs fast beneath.

tangle into mosshair
barkbodies compass an echo
imitation
creation repeating they are
the river and the banks they are
the forest joining
underground new
forms unfurling
in secret they are

Before they pull away, spent and cold, stiff with the wood that has held them, collecting themselves to themselves again, Jo feels it, the spark at her center, creation, the impossible newness that grows there, how it brightens.

They sit with their backs to the maple, listening to the sound of their breathing, listening to the currents as they go on around them.

Jo wants to remain in this pause. She does not want to move to leave it.

"I'm supposed to leave for a residency in a few days," Ness says, finally, slowly, as if words are hard to find, "Out east. It's on the ocean. The other one."

Jo nods. She was prepared for this, for the leaving. They are in a temporary space, passing through each other's lives and meeting for a moment.

Ness is looking at her intensely, searchingly, trying to find something hidden behind her eyes.

"Come with me."

"What?"

"Come with me. They let artists bring family or collaborators. We could keep working."

"Ness—"

"Jo. We weren't ready, back in college. We didn't know how

to do *this*. We were too young. But maybe, now…"

"What is *this*?"

"I think it's something that we've only ever just begun. I think we could give it a chance now, to become what it could be."

"Potential," Jo murmurs. She is caught in a wave of the past, that moment she stood on the sidewalk and watched Ness drive away.

"What we create together—it's something different than what we make alone. Can't you feel it? There's a kind of magic in it."

Jo thinks of what they have created, the dreams, the poems, the paintings, the strange power they seem to hold. Jo wonders what she would think of their creations now, the ones they made back then, if she could see them, if they had not been drown. She isn't sure what words to use, how to fully phrase the thought to ask the question.

"Do you think we caused it? In college. At your house. The flood."

She thinks Ness will laugh at her. But she nods instead.

"Maybe."

"That isn't possible."

"Oh, Jo," Ness says, putting her hand on Jo's cheek in a gentle kind of sympathy. "You're so realistic. You live in a world that isn't, though."

When Ness says the words, Jo understands, suddenly, what it is that they have made this time. Not a flood, but a seed. She can feel it inside her, burrowing.

"Ness—" she begins, wanting to tell her but not knowing the words for it.

Ness shakes her head. "Don't answer yet. I know it's a lot. I know you have a husband now. Just think about it."

"I will."

Ness smiles, warm as sunlight.

When they follow the narrow trail back, they realize what has made it, what it will become as fall moves into winter. In a month, when the rains begin in earnest, it will be a channel the rain takes to reach the river. They can both see it now, the way it will gush down in waves.

They fork at the edge of the river path. Jo almost invites Ness back with her to the motel. She wants to. It takes every bit of strength she has to let go of her hand. But she needs to think. The gravity of what she's done has only just begun to hold her.

"We'll get coffee later this morning," Ness is saying, "Then we can work at the studio."

Jo nods into the distance that is opening between them, a distance she knows she is making.

Alone, Jo is caught in the strangeness of the day, the way its rhythms try to right themselves despite it. The birds that had, an hour before, gone silent, are singing now. The world moves again, the eclipse fading to a memory of morning shadow.

Liam's car is parked in the motel parking lot right next to hers. She freezes when she sees it, remembers the missed call, the voicemail. Then she goes to it, finds him sitting in the front with his phone. In the moment before he sees her, she thinks he looks innocent and confused, like a mortal man lost in an enchanted forest who does not speak the language of the woods. She feels a tender protectiveness for him. She wishes she could save him from the life he's stumbled into.

When he looks up and sees her, he smiles, and she can tell he's been anxious. She's worried him.

He opens the car door, steps out. "I was calling. I'm sorry. I know you wanted space. I just wanted to see you."

The familiar of his voice almost settles her back to herself.

"You missed the eclipse."

"I know. This morning I woke up and thought I'd drive down and we could watch it together. Seemed a shame to miss seeing it with each other. But the traffic was gridlock."

"Did you see it?"

Liam nods. "It was incredible. I pulled over and stepped out to watch. It was like… seeing something impossible, like all the laws of the world were suspended."

"I know."

"I wish I'd seen it with you," he says.

They stand silently in the parking lot for a moment, remembering the sky. They have not touched each other. There is a wide, wary distance between them.

"So, what have you been up to down here this week?"

Jo shrugs, "Reminiscing."

"And writing," Liam adds.

Jo nods.

"Has it…helped?"

She is not sure what she should say to him. She cannot merge the reality standing before her with the reality of the days she has just moved through. She does not know which piece of each fits where. She knows she needs to tell him something but she does not know what or what words to use.

"Ness is here," she blurts out, knowing if she doesn't say it now, she never will.

It takes Liam a second to register the name, to remember why he knows it. "From college?"

"Yes. She's visiting. Showing work. Talking to art students. We've been catching up."

She can see the connections being made in Liam's mind. His face moves through each of them so visibly she wonders if he is capable of hiding anything, or if every minute feeling, every fragment of a thought, shows through.

"I didn't know you two were in touch."

"We haven't been, really. Just an occasional postcard."

Liam nods. "Is that why you came here? To see her?"

"Yes."

He doesn't ask the questions she thinks he will ask. But she thinks he knows what she hasn't said. She thinks he knows at least a part of it. She thinks she should say more. She thinks she should say everything. But she is watching the knowledge of betrayal descend in its weight onto him and she can't speak at all.

"Oh," he says, less of a word than a sound.

It is all dizzy unreality. Her stomach is heavy and light, rising and falling within her. There is a flutter inside her, an animal scurry, a rustle of leaves in her belly. The nausea comes quick. She is putting a shaking hand over her mouth, running to the door of her room, fumbling with the key, the doorknob, stumbling over the gray motel carpet. There is a brilliant flash of blank, the light and then the dark of it.

He is holding back her hair. She is hunched over the toilet, the taste of bile in her mouth. Her hand is still shaking. She is apologizing over and over. For the mess. For the trouble. For the way that her body has come out of her control.

52

Later that morning, they leave together. She just wants to go home, she tells him. The nausea hasn't left her, the dizziness. He wonders aloud if it is hormonal, her body recalibrating itself. She tells him she just wants to curl up and sleep in her own bed.

As she drives, following Liam's car up the highway, she is finally alone. She has split the world open. She is tunneling through while holding its two halves together. She can't keep it all in her mind at once—poems and paintings, dreams of Ness, selkie cones, eclipse seed unfurling, Liam, doctors, shots and fire, water gardens, home—none of it will stick. The fragments keep floating away from her. She can't make them into coherence.

She imagines Ness waiting at the café for her, giving up eventually to go to the studio, still sure that she will come. The reversal feels sickening, makes her doubly nauseous. But still, she does not call. She does not send a text. She will. Later. Once she is back home. Once she knows she cannot change her mind.

Part Three

Rime

1

Jo has been back for almost seven weeks when the home pregnancy test turns positive. She is surprised by her lack of surprise.

At first, a part of her, the more conscious part, the one that makes decisions, assumed the missed period was due to the fertility treatments, all those hormones still circling her reproductive system. So, she waited. But another part, some deeper self, knew, has known since that morning with Ness.

She finally bought the test after the second missed period. She picked it up at the grocery store, placed it in her basket with the bread and lettuce. She tried not to think about it at the counter when the checker gave her an encouraging smile as she scanned the box. She and Liam had had sex five times since her return. If she was pregnant, it would be his, of course. It couldn't be anyone else's. But that part of her that knows still knew.

In the bathroom, when she'd made a mess of it, trying to pee into the cup while her hands shook, finally giving up and just peeing directly onto the little stick, wiping it off with a sheet of toilet paper before setting it on the edge of the sink, thinking about how this process always seemed so simple and tidy in the movies, she set her timer and tried not to watch as the lines formed. She closed her eyes and, by the time the timer went off, Ness's face was all she saw there in the dark behind her lids.

Pregnant.

She'd known it already.

She tells Liam the result that night. She keeps the news uncertain. She says *might be, maybe, possible false positive.* Even though she knows. Even though she can sense something inside her, growing. But what if she is wrong? What if she is only imagining? She doesn't want to disappoint him.

"I made an appointment with the doctor so that we can know for sure," she tells him.

He nods. She can tell by his smile that he is trying to manage his hope. He reaches for her hand and wraps his fingers around hers.

"I'll go with you," he says.

Later that night, Jo tries to call Ness. Jo didn't call her the day she drove back home, following Liam's car. She hadn't known what to say, then, and Ness had never called her either. The silence between them felt sudden and astonishing, quietly cataclysmic, upending a whole world. It was also, she'd convinced herself, probably the right thing to do.

Now, these two months later, as she dials Ness's number, she isn't sure what she will say but she is pulled by the promise of her voice. Jo is sure what she wants to say would sound ridiculous. *I think I'm pregnant. I think it's yours.* But maybe Ness will understand it. Maybe Ness will know it already, the way Jo did, in that strange place inside her that knows things that are impossible to know.

There is no ringtone. Just an automated message about the number not being valid. She checks the digits, redials them, and gets the same.

It is college all over again. The disappearance, the being

left behind. Only this time, Jo knows it is her fault. This time, she herself has done the leaving.

The doctor tells them that this often happens when a couple stops trying. The pregnancy finally appears. "Almost like magic," she says and smiles, happy for them.

When they leave the office, Liam is beaming, his whole body glowing in a way Jo has never really seen before. There is a light coming off him. She thinks he has never looked so beautiful.

On the drive home, Liam begins to plan. They need to prepare. They need a crib, and baby clothes. The baby will need something to wear. He looks at the map on his phone, drives them to a baby store where he picks out a newborn sized onesie, a tiny pair of socks, and a baby blanket.

"A summer baby," he says, eying a rack of tiny sun hats, and Jo is surprised by the dreamy quality that has entered his voice. She realizes how long it has been since she's heard this particular tone from him. It takes her back to before those years of fertility worry, before all the counting and the tests and the shots wearied him into their realism. Now, his words pull her back to that time when they held all the magic of possibility between them.

2

But, almost ten weeks into the pregnancy, Jo begins to worry about Liam's enthusiasm.

"It's early yet," she tells him when he wants to break the news to all his colleagues at work. Her mind is a blur of statistics: chance of miscarriage after thirty-five, risk of genetic abnormality, risk of preeclampsia, hemorrhage, stillbirth, premature birth. The numbers scroll like a constant news ticker at the edge of her brain, and alongside them, those other numbers: degrees of planetary warming within the next ten years, fifteen, twenty; increased rate and severity of wildfires; impact of wildfire smoke on rates of childhood asthma; rate of species extinction; rate of ecosystem collapse; rate of land loss, storm severity, catastrophic flood. If this potential becomes a child becomes an adult, how many years, what age, before the world becomes unrecognizable, what age before inhospitable, what age before uninhabitable? She has, she realizes, begun to imagine the future mapped onto a lifetime that extends past her own.

3

Jo scours the internet for hints of Ness and finds nothing new. Ness doesn't keep social media. She never did. She doesn't have a contact form on her website. She makes herself surprisingly untraceable through sheer neglect of web presence.

Jo finds a short write up of the art show in the university paper. It has a list of the students who showed their work and a line about Ness, about how her paintings were "eerily magnetic." There is a picture of the tree/woman painting and Jo wonders what has happened to it, if it is still sitting on the alumni wall or if Ness has it with her now, wherever she is, tucked away with the rest of her old work. Jo thinks about the work they were making together, wonders if Ness is still working on it, or if she set it aside or destroyed it when Jo disappeared on her.

Ness never wanted children. Liam always has. Jo suspects the end result will be the same whether Ness knows or not. But she needs Ness to know. She needs Ness to know whether it is possible to magic up a baby from treeroots and riversound and moonsun.

Now, when she looks at Ness's work, she feels a tug inside her that isn't from her, as if the creature growing in her is drawn to the paintings. She puts a hand on her naval, sensing currents within currents.

4

The first ultrasound is like peering through a window into a space so deep inside her she does not know the terrain of it. The technician moves the scanner over her belly, pressing down, sliding along the cold gel, revealing a whole hidden landscape. It is all there on the screen, mapped out in silver and gray and black with a tiny creature right there at the center. The creature moves in liquid wriggles, shapeshifts right before her eyes from tadpole to mushroom to bulb to infant in miniature. Theirs is a liquid existence. They don't yet know what they will be. Amorphous and unhardened, they could be anything.

She wonders if the creature feels the scanner pressing down, wonders if the disturbance of this looking frightens them. She tries to think comfort into the silvergray world of the screen, into this place that is unreachable. She wishes she could hold the embryo in her arms. Now, at the core of her, they are so impossibly far, so easily lost. She feels so keenly, now, how their liquid life will end in currents that could pull them closer or push them forever away.

5

Jo cannot write. For weeks, she has tried and failed to find the flow of words again. She worries that she left them by the river, worries they stuck in that moment just after totality, scattered with those little moonshadows beneath the tree beside the water. A sacrifice, perhaps, for this other kind of making. Life for life. Creation for creation.

Or maybe, she left them with Ness. It is possible, she thinks, that the writing only works when she is with her, that it is just an offshoot from the spark of Ness's art. What if, Jo begins to fear, the words were never really hers to begin with?

6

Jo isn't sure when the pregnancy begins to show. Liam says he can tell, that there is a little bump where her belly used to lie flatter. Her pregnancy app tells her that at twelve weeks, her uterus will be the size of a grapefruit, will push up over her pelvic bone and into her abdomen, jostling for a place between organs.

Jo wonders what that movement will be like for the creature growing there, a journey of inches, the farthest they have travelled in their short pre-life. She has begun to put a hand over her belly when she thinks of them, as if they are already a baby she can soothe.

7

At some point, she can't say exactly when, she notices the way the world begins to bend toward her. She first sees it on a walk, when a flock of migrating robins doesn't move from the path as she passes. At first, she thinks, they are busy seeking worms in the ground in the rain. Then one flits right past her ear. Another stops and stares at her and she is sure that they are curious. She notices it next in the squirrels, the way they run right up to her even though she is not carrying any food for them. She begins to come eye to eye with them when she passes beneath trees. From the branches, they swish their furry tails and chirrup with startling intention.

8

At twelve weeks, Jo tells her boss at work that she is pregnant, she is told that the company maternity leave is a six-week disability policy paid at half-salary, with the first week unpaid.

"But you can absolutely take as much additional unpaid time off as you need," her boss tells her. "We're a really family-friendly company."

She nods, tries not to let the shock show too clearly on her face as she says, "Thank you."

Walking back to her desk, she is astonished she never checked the parental leave policy before, that she knew only that they had one, that she trusted the "family-friendly company" line at her interview, assuming it would be enough. She tells herself she should feel lucky having any time off at all. But all she feels is a searing rage that will not dissipate, that only grows as she drafts taglines for a new sustainable wellness hotel chain whose main claim to environmentalism is that the guest rooms have potted plants. She makes a list of words that can refer to both human and planetary health: bloom, regenerate, sustain, flourish, thrive. As she looks at the list, the familiar dizziness washes over her. She thought she'd left the morning sickness weeks ago, but here it is again, the bile stinging the back of her throat.

That weekend, she and Liam make a list of numbers. If they use her vacation time, Jo can afford a nine week leave. Liam has no paternity leave at his nonprofit job, but he's saved up three weeks of vacation by not taking any for over a year. Daycare won't accept infants under ten weeks old.

"So, I'll take my first two weeks when the baby is born," Liam says, "and then my last week when you go back to work, and we'll be fine. That'll get us to ten weeks."

"Right," Jo says. "Okay. Perfect."

She tries not to think past those first ten weeks, tries not to imagine how it will be to leave an infant in the hands of a stranger to return to a job doing active harm with, and to, words. It isn't hard not to think of. She can hardly imagine the infant in the first place. Right now, there is still just the potential, shapeshifting and tenuous, hopeful, growing inside her.

9

Liam begins setting up daycare visits.

"The waitlists are over half a year long," he tells her when she tries to tell him it is too soon. "And to get on them we have to go tour the centers. I know, it's ridiculous."

The evening of the first visit, they meet after work at the daycare around the corner from Jo's office. It is perfect, she thinks as she walks through the cold of the dusk, she could come to the baby on her lunch breaks. If they were sick, if there was an emergency, in a disaster, in a flood or a fire or earthquake, even if the city shut down, she could run here in minutes.

She mentions this to Liam when she meets him at the entrance, and he frowns at her.

"You shouldn't be thinking like that," he says. "I mean, the lunch part, that's great, really great. But you're not going to have to run here like you're in a disaster movie. That won't happen."

"We don't know that," she murmurs as they join the line of expectant parents picking up nametags inside. There are so many of them, at least twenty just in the hall.

"How many spots did you say they had opening up this year?" she asks Liam who has done the research, who has set up all the daycare visits.

"Three to five. Most of the infant spots go to families who already have kids going here."

When they get to the room, there are even more parents. They fill up the corners, standing around the toy bins, perched on the colorful carpets. Once they have all gathered, the daycare director explains their childcare philosophy while the staff hands out booklets on child development. Jo can't keep track of all the tenants they mention, all the scientific sources they cite. It is overwhelming, all the things that should and should not be done when caring for a child. The director explains that they never use the word "no" in their center, that they always distract the children when they are biting or hitting, that they try to avoid negative words that create negative feelings. Jo feels a sinking sense of inadequacy. She has not done the research. She does not know what this creature inside her will need. She does not understand all the subtle ways that she will fail them, the cumulative impact of all the "no's" that she will pile on their small ears in her attempts to save them from danger.

At the end of the talk, they are taken downstairs to the infant room. They are currently, the director explains, in one of the larger toddler rooms, made for rambling and play. Upstairs are the rooms for older children, filled with elaborate play structures and art tables. Downstairs, in the basement, in the infant rooms, there are no windows. There are tiny mats piled neatly in one corner and a sink and refrigerator in the other. The carpet is green and the walls are painted with murals of clouds. It is a pretty room, a tidy room, a dim room.

"We take the infants outside most days once they're all a bit older," the director explains, apologetically, when one parent mentions the lack of natural light. "The first months are usually pretty hectic, and it can be hard to have everyone ready at once, but we prioritize getting them out in the fresh air."

That's when Jo begins to imagine it, how small and helpless the baby will be when she hands them over to these carers, who are so well-educated and so expert and precise in their care, but who are not her, who are not Liam, who are doing their best for a group of crying ten-week-olds who do not understand why they are left here in a room without windows all day.

The group is shuffled back upstairs and handed clipboards on the way out to give their names for the waitlist. Jo leaves Liam to fill out the form while she steps outside into the cold night. There are tears pricking at her eyes, sharp as frost, as she thinks about how it will be, how she will be only blocks away but how the blocks will create an impossible distance. She will sit at her desk and write her pointless copy while her child is in this place, growing without her. And for a moment, she wishes she could keep them here inside her, safe and close and warm, held in this realm of liquid possibility before the world will harden them.

10

She sits diligently at her desk every night after work, taking an hour to try at the poetry. But it is impossible to find words in the midst of this. Her mind is foggy and imprecise.

"Baby brain. It comes to best of us. But it'll pass," one of her coworkers reassured her upon catching three typos in one paragraph of Jo's copy after word of her pregnancy got around the office and all the women started asking her questions about her breasts, her digestion, her pelvic floor, her back, her feet, her sleep.

Perhaps, the words have hidden somewhere, away from the well-intentioned prying of colleagues and friends, away from the prodding of doctors, away from the intricate planning with Liam. She begins to wonder if, away from all of that, even just for a few days, she could find them again and keep them with her this time, if the poetry just needs her to drop out of the buzz of this world for a while to dip back into its different rhythms.

She doesn't plan it so much as dream it: a long weekend, maybe half a week, alone.

11

The ice storm is preceded by snow. It falls in the night, becomes a quiet glisten in the still-bright morning. When Jo wakes, she stares out the window, enchanted.

The world slows with the snow. The unplowed streets are mostly empty of cars. Schools close and everyone who can is working from home. By midmorning, the children have emerged with their sleds, heading toward the park and the empty school fields. Jo allows herself to imagine her own child enjoying the snow, the way they will tromp through it in bright boots, the little snowmen they will build beneath the trees with rocks for eyes and twigs for hair, how they will smile up at her, bright as the light of ice crystals.

Liam, feeling festive, makes them both hot chocolate at breakfast. They take their time over their oatmeal and eggs, allow the work emails to pile up as they laugh, warm in the winter weather.

"I was thinking," Jo begins, believing now might be a time to bring it up, when they are together and relaxed, "what if I took a little time off from work and went on a small trip. To rest. To write. Just a few days. Before the baby comes."

"But I thought you were using all your vacation time for leave," Liam says.

"That was the plan. But maybe, I could take a few more unpaid days."

"That's not what we budgeted."

"I know. But how much difference will a few days make, really?"

Liam is frowning. She can see him debating how much resistance to give. She knows he knows she will do it, whether he wants her to or not. She can see that he doesn't want her to, that there is something more to it than the budgeting that is concerning him.

"Why don't we go together?" he suggests. "A short vacation. Just the two of us. Before the baby makes us three."

He is smiling, but there is an edge to it. He doesn't want her running off again.

He has not mentioned Ness once since they returned home. She assumes he has inferred it all, that he knows she is a cheater, that he has somehow excused or forgiven her, or will, at some point. But they have not spoken the words of it aloud. The silence around it is tenuous and necessary. The words, if let go, would so quickly run out of their control.

"That sounds nice," she says, meeting his smile with hers and feeling the falseness of it. And it would be nice, a vacation with her husband, some time away together before the baby comes. But it is not what she meant.

All that next night, they hear the rain. It freezes as it falls, tapping at the windows, clattering over the roof. The dancing of a million sharp and tiny feet.

That morning, they wake to it. The trees shimmer with ice that has grown an inch thick, encasing even the smallest of twigs, wrapping itself around every fir needle. The snowy ground glistens glassy in the dawn.

When Jo ventures outside, she slips and almost falls on the walkway. There is nowhere that is not iced over. The morning is beautiful and treacherous.

They stay home again, this time, more anxiously. Everywhere is closed. No cars dare the streets. Even bus routes cease to run. The roads are sheets no plow can clear. The city is frozen over.

Jo finds Liam in the kitchen, surveying the cupboards.

"I didn't get to the grocery store this weekend when I should have, but we'll be fine," he says when he sees her. "We have a bunch of canned food if the ice lasts awhile. We're a little low on coffee, but we can manage without that."

"There's the ultrasound tomorrow," Jo reminds him.

"We should try to reschedule. I don't think we'll be able to drive in this. The weather says it won't melt for at least a few days."

"I'll call this morning. Maybe see if they can get us in later this week."

"Great," Liam says, and he puts his arm around her protective and reassuring. "We'll be alright. The ice will melt soon. It'll give us time to plan our trip."

Jo smiles up at him, feeling the distance between them begin to solidify.

13

Days later, the freeze still grips the city in strange stasis. The top layers of ice melt and refreeze each day, growing thicker every night. All across the city, trees break and pull down powerlines. Their doctor's office has cancelled all upcoming appointment due to power loss. Countless work colleagues dial into meetings from area hotels, having lost power in their homes with no signs of regaining heat for days. The sky has turned slate gray, closing in around them.

Jo tries to work, but she is constantly distracted by head-lines. She prints out the articles and pins them to the walls around her desk, news of the freeze joining her ever-growing collage of environmental devastation.

Freezing Rain Blankets Region

Hundreds of Thousands Without Power—Largest Outage in City History

Coldest Day on Record

Trees Topple in Freeze

There is a picture of a large maple downtown that has fall-en into an apartment building, felled beneath the weight of their own icy branches. No people are injured but the tree is dead. The article warns readers not to walk in wooded areas, to beware of heavy limbs.

Liam walks in as she is pinning up the image of the downed tree, all the shattered ice lying beneath it on the sidewalk, sharp like frosted glass. He sighs when he sees it.

"We should take all that down before the baby comes," he says, gesturing to the wall of them, all those terrifying headlines and apocalyptic images.

"We should?"

"You don't need this kind of stress right now. And a child shouldn't grow up with this always right there in front of them. It gives *me* nightmares."

"You think we should hide what's happening?"

Liam sighs, tries again. "I'm not saying hide it. Of course we don't look away. But you can't put the whole weight of climate change on a little kid. They need to have a childhood."

"It's going to be the fabric of their childhood. It's the world we're bringing them into. Summers of fire. Winters of ice. Hurricanes. Tornados. Storms. Drought. It's already on them."

"So, you just sit here staring at it and doing nothing? Is that what you think we should do?"

It is the nothing that stings her, the lack of the doing.

"You think your community gardens are going to save the planet?" she asks him. The cruelty of the question tastes bitter in her mouth.

"I think giving people the opportunity to grow their own food, teaching them about the systems they're a part of, I think that's not nothing."

"Poetry isn't nothing."

"Isn't it, though? You used to publish them, but now, you won't even show them to me anymore."

"It isn't about that."

"Then what is it about? You sit here with all this horror in solitude and, what, write poems about it? And then you just hide them away? Who is that helping?"

She can't describe it, the making of a poem, the way it is important, how the making is the part that's essential. Like a spell or a prayer, a reaching across impossible, impassable boundaries. A more than human magic.

"It's how I deal with it," she tells him, simply, even though she knows that is not right. That is not what she is trying to say.

"This," he gestures to the pictures again, "isn't dealing with it. This is wallowing. It's almost like you like it."

"What?"

"Destruction."

"You think I like destruction?" Jo asks. The argument is getting away from them, turning dangerous. She sees Liam making a decision before he speaks.

"Yes. I think there's a part of you that wants to watch things be destroyed, that maybe even wants to destroy them yourself. I've thought about it a lot. What else could it be? This wall? That trip? I think there must be something in you that wants to destroy our marriage, the family we're trying to make. All of it."

"What makes you think that?" she asks, trying to keep her voice even, trying not to be destructive.

"You know what."

She thinks, at first, that he won't say the words. She can play it out in her mind, the way they could back away from this moment. She would nod and say, "Yes." And say, "You're right. I'll take the pictures down." And he would let that be the end of it. For now. They would put the conversation off for later like they have been. Maybe years later. They'd get wrapped up in the pregnancy again and then the baby. And maybe, by the time they spoke it, it would feel so far away, so much a thing from another time, a time before their family, that it would hardly matter. Maybe, when they looked at it directly, it would no longer feel real to them, or painful, and they would almost laugh at the strangeness of their pre-parent selves. She thinks she could end this moment now, could steer them both away from the words Liam is so close to speaking. Instead, she pushes forward.

"Yes. I know what. But I think you need to say it."

Liam sighs and lifts his hands as if he is trying to hold something. Finding nothing there, he lets them drop.

"You slept with Ness, right?"

"Yes. Just once. It wasn't to hurt you."

Liam's head gives a sharp nod, a curtailed contained motion, as if he is trying to put a thought away and be done with it.

"I can't believe you did that. You just left. Right in the middle of things. You just left. For…an ex-girlfriend?"

"I'm sorry," Jo says. And it is half true. She is sorry for the betrayal, sorry for causing him pain, though, even seeing that pain now, the way he is holding it inside him, she would not undo it. She would not take that morning back.

"I think the baby's hers." She says it quickly, before she can think, before the impossibility of the statement can catch up to her. The moment the words are said, she feels the most intense relief. Once released, she understands how long and how tightly she has held them.

She knows that Liam is right. She has destroyed them. Their marriage. The family they thought they were making. He will leave her now. She will raise the child alone. But at least, it will have been honest. She will have said the impossibly true thing. She will look up from the rubble one day and wonder how she could have made it. But now, she is caught in the sharp solace that comes with the finality of breaking.

"Jo, that isn't possible," Liam is saying, and his voice has moved into a register of forced calm. There is a tension beneath it, so much more frightening than any shouting or crying could be. It is the sound of her husband believing she is crazy.

"I know," Jo says, matching his calm with a steady stubbornness, an immovability growing between them. "I understand that. But it's true all the same."

Liam is shaking his head. His eyes are wide with disbelief. "Who are you?"

She feels a rustle inside her in response, a shift of bark and leaves.

"I'm me," she tells him.

He shakes his head again. "No. You're something else. You're not who I thought I was married to."

He doesn't look at her when he leaves the room. He shuts the door gently, so quietly she almost isn't sure he has gone.

14

That evening, she steps outside into heavy gray. Sky. Ground. A painting seeped of color.

The sequoia's limbs droop downward, rimed with frost, brushing the top of the garage with their graygreen glisten.

Crows wheel overhead, cawing between heavy, burdened trees, landing and alighting, their calls amplifying into icy echoes. They are wildness itself. They are the heart of the world released into the sky, sharp and dark and reeling. They are the only movement in the terrible stillness.

15

She sleeps on the pullout couch in the guestroom that will become the child's room. The crib sits in the corner, waiting for assembly. She tries not to think as she pulls an extra quilt around her. They still have power. She has turned the heat up. But the house holds the cold of the air, of the glassy world encased. She sleeps immediately and more completely than she has in weeks.
limbs wood into her dreams

shatter

glassfall melt soft

taps on a window of snow
crackling

warning
build
electric
build
irrevocable
final break
proceed
the fall
of bark
explode
the ice

178

16

She wakes to the sound of water. It drips from the roof, the trees, the powerlines. The melt is fast and full.

Liam is still in their room when she puts on her boots to step outside. She walks down a street filled with shattered ice and puddles and softening snow and broken tree limbs. They are everywhere, the fallen branches, their pieces spread out on the road: needles and twigs, bark and shattered wood. Across the street, the neighbors are pulling a large branch out of their driveway. "Just missed the car by a foot!" they shout to her, laughing at their luck. Two blocks down, a family is hauling what looks like half a tree out of the middle of the street. Everywhere, the wreckage. She stops counting the trees with visible breaks, whole pieces of them pulled apart with the weight of the freeze. She begins to fear the spring. The way she will know who has survived when they begin to bud or don't. She imagines a summer without the green of leaves to shield them from the sharp jagged ways of the sun.

When she returns home, Liam has taken his car to drive into work. He has left a note to tell her that he will be working late, that she does not need to wait up for him.

But she does wait up for him. She waits, thinking of all the women he works with, how he mostly works with women in his underpaid nonprofit field. All those gardeners. All those healthy active good women who take positive action, who address the problems of the world in concrete steps. Women who nurture—plants, communities, policies. Women who grow things, who reach, uncomplicatedly, toward the light.

She thinks she should be jealous, imagining what her husband might be doing. But she finds she is, perhaps, relieved. It would be fair, she thinks. It might be good for him. It would balance things again. It might help him understand. And in the end, she knows it would bring him back to her. She finds herself almost hoping he is beginning an affair.

17

In the weeks that follow, Jo cannot stop writing. She sleeps on the couch in the room with the unmade crib. Liam leaves for work early and returns home late, hardly looking at her when they pass in the kitchen. Jo moves through a world that is doubled, the unreal and the real mapping over each other. Leafwhisper moonsong raintap and the waiting for the phantom feelings of kicks that she knows will come soon. She carries layers of secrets inside her.

Jo isn't sure what the fragments of poems will become. She writes them anyway, snatches of verse moving into her mind while she types out her work emails, shops at the grocery store, rides the bus, sleeps. The words are everywhere, crowding in. They come fastest when she walks the wooded paths by their house or when she sits under the backyard sequoia or in that in-between space when she is first coming out of her dreams or first falling into them. She keeps a notebook beside her when she sleeps to try to catch threads that fray faster than her waking mind can catch them.

She is writing toward something. The cracking trees. The burning woods. The freeze. The way the thing that grows inside her rearranges her, shifting her center, displacing organs she thought were immoveable.

18

Jo tries to write Liam a letter. She tries, with the words, to be clear. But the words get away from her. Wind into something else. When she reads them over again, she finds a poem inside them, a poem that is not meant for Liam.

It is as if a force is moving through her and pushing everything else out of the way. She can't focus her mind on her marriage or her job or all the chores that have piled up around the house. The words. The creature growing in her. She can sense them rumbling together. She has not felt a definite kick yet, but she thinks she has felt the movement already, maybe, a murmur beginning just under her bellybutton.

The poems are strange creatures. They wander into each other, overweaving at the roots. Sometimes she cannot tell where one poem ends and another begins. They tangle like a forest, leafy and bursting with undergrowth. They make shadows deep and wide.

She begins, in the mornings before she leaves work, in the evenings while Liam is staying out late, to leave little gifts by his side of the bed: a sprig of fir, a smooth stone, a little pile of dried flower petals. It is an animal thing, she realizes, this strange token leaving. It is the language of crows and cats. She tries to translate it back into human, leaves a bar of chocolate, a notecard with the simple words *I love you.*

19

Every morning, just as the sun begins to rise, Jo walks across the cold grass and sits beneath the sequoia. Perched amidst their roots, she watches the sky glow orange and pink as her breath curls around her. She brings a notebook so she can tangle with the words. She hears them in the trunk of the tree, the roots reaching beneath her, the branches as they whisper in the breezes. Sometimes, she startles a wandering raccoon who goes still on their hind legs and stares at her, or a foraging squirrel who hesitates when they notice her presence. But the more often the animals find her there, the less afraid they become. After a few weeks, the squirrel begins to pause beside her, looking up. The raccoon rests less than a yard from her hand. It is as if she has become a tree herself, an unobtrusive aspect of the morning. She can feel it—
     the quiet of rings
        circling strong at her
center
 In those moments just before the dawn, as the colors shift from night to day, she does not experience the cold. In that time of in between, she feels herself as something else, moving into different rhythms, almost shifting shape.

20

She begins to lose her place in time. Days of the week feel uncertain. She will glance at some crows loitering outside her window and find that an hour has passed. She moves with the sunset and sunrise, misses a whole day of work without realizing it and has to plead illness retroactively. But she writes.

One morning, as she sits beneath the sequoia with her notebook before work—she has set an alarm on her phone so she does not forget again—Liam comes out of the house carrying two mugs of coffee. They have hardly spoken in weeks, days, years? He is a stranger striding toward her.

He hands her a mug, says, in his practical voice, "We need to make some decisions."

Jo nods, tracing the edges of the mug with fingers she did not realize were cold until they held the warmth of it.

"I never did anything to deserve this," he tells her. "I've always been a good husband. I've never done anything but love you."

Jo watches the steam spiraling up from her coffee and tries to keep herself in this moment of her marriage, here, now, sitting under the sequoia, Liam standing there, his face cast in shadow by the sunrise. But she feels tendrils of words reaching out to her, thrumming up from under earth, humming through her back where bones touch the bark of the tree.

"I know," she tells the good husband who is waiting for her to give him something human.

"Then why did you cheat on me?"

Jo tries to ignore the annoyance creeping in at her edges. The word isn't the right one. It's a blunt word. A cheap word. It can't contain her or Ness or any of it. "It wasn't about you," she hears herself saying and knows those aren't the words he needs from her.

She can't see the look on his face for the sun as he takes a step back from her asking, "How could you say that?"

Jo shakes her head, trying to clear the steam and the thrum and glint of the sun on the clouds. "Can we talk about this later?" she asks. "I'm writing."

Liam widens his eyes at her. "I don't understand you," he says.

"I don't understand you either," she tells him just before he turns back to the house, leaving her to the chill of the morning.

She returns to her notebook.

21

Jo is sure Liam will skip their next appointment. So sure, that she does not send him a text from work or from the bus to remind him of it. But when she arrives at the doctor's office, she finds him in the waiting room. He looks up at her with a pained expression. She is not sure if he wants her to sit beside him or not. She takes the seat next to his.

"I'm glad you're here," she tells him.

"I keep my promises," he says.

He doesn't say anything more. The silence between them grows impossible. She cannot find the voice to cross it.

Instead, she looks around the room at the many couples and lone waiters. They are all at various stages of pregnancy, some visibly pregnant and some not. Jo realizes, as she looks around her, that she is at the midpoint, halfway through it, a long way off, but also a long way in. In a matter of months, there will be a child.

At the ultrasound, Liam sits beside her in the usual chair, but he does not look at her, does not touch her. They watch the scan come into form on the screen. The doctor describes what they see, but they know already, the shape has become so well-defined, so human.

"Do you want to know the sex?" the doctor asks.

The question surprises Jo. It surprises her, most of all, that she has not thought of it before now. When she has seen the potential in her mind, it has not been as a boy or girl, but simply as a child, as her child.

"No," Jo tells the doctor, quick and decisive. Liam jostles his confusion beside her.

"We want it to be a surprise," he says, apologetically, as if he is trying to cover up something embarrassing that she has done.

Liam offers her a ride back to work. In the car, she tries to explain it.

"It just doesn't feel right," she says. "For this child, for what I can feel of them, that kind of gendering. It's the first thing anyone asks when they find out I'm pregnant. And it always seems so wrong. Boy or girl. And then they tell me how boy babies are all energy and girl babies are so placid. And I keep thinking that we're bringing this child into a world of collapse already, we're giving them this inheritance of extinction and ongoing catastrophe. They'll already be trapped on a dying world. Do we have to trap them in gender too? Can't we give them something more than that? Something more than we had? Something, maybe, hopeful? Could we give them more space to become in, more room to create for themself?"

She expects confusion or even an argument. She does not expect him to say what he does.

"I guess that makes sense," he tells her, watching the road. "Some of the parents at work have been talking about doing that—or, well, trying anyway. Let the kid define their own gender. Our child wouldn't be the only one at their daycare. It wouldn't be that weird. Not here, anyway. Not at this point. Let's keep talking about it."

And as he speaks, Jo feels an immense love for him, for the way he is always surprising her with his capacity.

22

The night after the ultrasound, when Jo goes to the guest room to sleep, she finds Liam there, assembling the crib.

"I don't know what you want," he says, holding the frame of the crib together upside-down while he tightens the screws with the tiny Allen wrench that came in the box.

"I want to be a family," she says, and she knows that is true. She knows she does not want to leave him. She does not want him to leave her. She knows she wants to raise the child together. She has always wanted to. Whatever else she wants as well, she knows that she wants that.

"That's what I want too." He looks up at her, now, and she expects his eyes to look angry or stern. But they are only afraid.

"I'm not trying to destroy that," she tells him. "I'm really not."

He nods, sets the crib upright and walks around it, checking for stability, tightening the last screws with his hands that seem always so solidly sure of themselves. "I just don't understand what happened. I don't understand why you did it."

"I can't explain it," Jo tells him, wishing she could find the words for what she and Ness hold between them, the world they have sometimes made together. But it is beyond her ability to describe it. The words, the reason, will not come.

"Because I tried," Liam tells her. "Cheating. Sleeping with someone else. I couldn't do it. I can't do it. It isn't in me."

189

He is kneeling there next to the crib, and she thinks he looks angry and cruel and helpless. Her breath catches in her throat and stays there, lost, forgetting the path to her lungs.

"Do you really think I'm not the father?"

He is not looking at her. He is turned toward the crib. She cannot see his face. She notices how small the room seems now, how much larger the crib is than she expected.

"Of course you're the father," she says. "But Ness is the mother too."

She is caught between the truths of it. It is a space she knows she has to hold.

He stops testing the crib, looks back at her in wonder or maybe in fear. "Jo, the way you see things sometimes…"

She watches him flounder for words and waits for the judgement that doesn't come. A quiet space opens between them. The realities overlay each other. The many-ness of parentage. She does not know how it resolves. She thinks it may be irresolvable, that she will spend her life in this in-between knowledge, the meeting place of possibilities. Nessmother, Liamfather, a child begotten by trees and water, woven out of roots and soil and currents where the moon meets the sun.

"This is our child," she says and the *our* is expansive, human and not, real and impossible. This *our* is the place she will live in.

There is a ripple inside her, the creature reaching. They are reaching out to Liam from that inaccessible place deep within her. They are stuck behind her skin and wanting.

"And you really haven't spoken to her since the eclipse?" Liam asks. She can hear the wariness in his question and the hope.

"She's gone," Jo tells him, and the reality of the loss is an ocean she cannot touch for fear of drowning.

She sees her pain reflected in his face as he sets the crib in its final spot and crosses the room to wrap his arms around her and the creature inside her.

That's when they both feel it, unmistakable, the kick.

23

It is in the spring that she begins to dream of Ness.

Ness is searching through old trunks and boxes, opening each one and pulling out a dusty fur. She holds each fur in her hands and shakes her head, sadly, every time. The furs pile up next to her as she discards them. The pile grows taller than Ness is. Jo thinks she sees it start to wobble. She worries it will topple over onto Ness, bury her in dead animal skins. She wants to shout to her. But Jo is not inside the dream. She is just an observer. She cannot speak her warning. Ness keeps opening boxes.

24

Jo and Liam spend a weekend setting up the nursery. They are cautious with each other, quieter than usual, all shy glances and encouraging smiles. Liam installs a set of shelves while Jo puts up wall decals of trees and birds and flowers, shadows of the spring that brightens outside the windows.

Jo cannot force herself to stay inside for long. More and more frequently, she is drawn out to the yard, on walks, into errands she does not really need to run. She cannot sit still at her desk at work for more than ten minutes at a time. The spring makes her restless, makes the creature inside her wriggle and kick and squirm. They both desperately need to get out.

25

As the weather warms, waking, unable to sleep again, Jo creeps from her bed, leaving Liam to solitary dreaming, and finds herself outside in the middle of the night. Beneath the sequoia, gazing up at the moon glowing through branches of needles, she feels her body changing in ways she cannot fully understand. Inside, the will-be-child grows. Outside, she is a strengthening in a kind of multiplicity, tendrils of her self moving outward, a reaching. Still, her back against the tree, she is unconfined.

When she half-sleeps beside the sequoia, resting her head against their bark and closing her eyes on the night, she dreams

    trees beget people

        humans emerge

            uprooting fingers

                digging up from under

                    ground mycelium mud

                        reaching bones aglow

                            the creature turns inside her

                                  sure as a ripple of wood

26

She is aware of every move they make in her belly, all the sharp tiny kicks and punches, all the liquid undulations. When too much time goes by without a movement, she begins to count minutes. She is constantly alert for danger coming from without or within.

27

Sometimes, she startles Liam when, waking early, he peeks his head out the back door, groggy and searching for her when she isn't in the bed beside him. The third time he finds her there, after, when she has come back inside to become solely human again, as they make their coffee in the kitchen, he asks, "Are you okay out there? It's so cold this early."

"I'm fine," she tells him.

When he realizes she is writing again, he asks if he can read the poems sometime.

She shakes her head. "I don't even know what they are yet. I don't think they would make a lot of sense at this point."

But really, she can't imagine him reading them. He has almost never read her poems, only the handful that she published in journals years ago before they were married. Even then, she could tell he hadn't really understood them. He'd told her all the nature imagery made him feel like he was "taking a relaxing walk."

She fears, if she shows him what she is writing now, he will be disturbed. Or, even worse, he will tell her again how pretty her poems are.

28

Jo is never not at the doctor's office. The appointments grow closer and closer together. Every two weeks shifts to every week shifts to every few days.

The doctor tells her this is normal, this level of monitoring. The baby could survive outside her now and so, on each visit, they are weighing the safety of giving the baby more time or, if it were to look like something was beginning to go wrong, taking the baby out early.

"Don't worry," the doctor assures her. "We're not seeing anything wrong. You're both doing great."

But still, Jo worries. What if her insides turn treacherous? What if the delicate ecosystem of pregnancy begins to break down around them? What if the baby would be safer out in the world than locked in the center of her? What if the doctor can't get them out in time?

29

By the last weeks of her pregnancy, Jo has a notebook full of poems. She thinks they are like the voices of trees and moss and stone. They are messages to the future child, the child who will grow up in a shapeshifting world of accelerated change, who may never know a time when the foundations of form felt stable. She isn't sure that anyone else will like the poems. But they feel true to her. They feel like the truest words she has ever written. She wishes she could show them to Ness.

Instead, she puts them in the drawer of her desk to whisper to themselves in the dark.

30

The night before her due date, Jo dreams she is standing on a familiar shore with Ness. The ghost forest surrounds them, the dead tree roots and stumps glowing silver in the moonlight.

In her hands, Ness holds a silver fur. It glows like frost, prickly and cold and beautiful.

"I found it," Ness tells her.

"What is it?" Jo asks, her voice comes out slow and wavering, like it is trying to speak underwater.

"My skin," Ness says. Her mouth is next to Jo's ear and Jo can feel her breath like a cold breeze across her neck.

"Come with me," Ness says. She is looking out at the water, now, dark under the moon, full of shadows beneath its glistening surface.

"Come with me," Ness says again as she drapes the fur over her shoulders. But Jo cannot move. Her feet are growing roots, digging down through the sand, fast and sure. Her body has already begun to bark over.

Ness is drifting away from her, as if she is already being pulled out by currents of ocean, her shape wavering between human and something else.

Jo reaches an arm toward her. The arm is a branch growing leaves.

The distance expands until Jo can hardly see Ness, until she is only a glint of silver on the dark of the waves.

The dead trees of the ghost forest grow up around her, threaded through with glinting. Their branches hide the moon.

Jo smells the smoke before she sees the glow of fire. It spreads across the ghost forest, jumping from tree to tree, a memory of past meeting a memory of future.

She thinks of the cones that open in the flames, seeding the ground after burning, the new green unfurling up through apocalypse.

She cannot move. Her branches wave in the warming wind, waiting to alight.

Jo feels the kick inside her—mousescurry, stonethrow, leafdrop, foxclaw. What kind of creature, she wonders, do a selkie and a tree make together? What shapes will this baby hold inside them? How will those shapes open? When?

31

On her due date, Jo has an appointment with the doctor. There is no sign of imminent labor.

"It's alright," the doctor tells her. "First births are often late."

They put her on the induction schedule for the following week anyway.

"Just in case," the doctor says. "A week late is perfectly normal. If we start to get past that, that's when I'll get concerned."

The doctor assures her that she can always move the induction appointment if she wants to wait longer.

"It's easier to cancel at the last minute than to fit you in the schedule at the last minute."

Jo smiles, trying to look reassured.

At Jo's next appointment, three days after her due date, when she still shows no signs of going into labor, her doctor tells her to start taking her leave from work right away.

"Stress can delay labor," the doctor says. "I'll write you a note to give them. Doctor's orders. You need to relax."

Jo laughs. Her mind is a constant buzz, clanging with worry, jangling with nerves. She has never felt less able to relax. But she follows the doctor's orders and sends the note to her boss and stays home, counting the days of her leave that are wasted, days she will not get to spend with her infant on the other side of the birth.

She spends the days monitoring the soon-to-be baby inside her. She frets at every movement and every long gap in motion. Always, in the back of her mind, the question: what if they never make it out? Now, so close to the end of things, what if she fails them? Once they are out, she knows they will be safe. They will have Liam with all his strength and care and steadiness. But, until then, they are stuck with her, only her, reliant on her hidden internal ecologies.

It is almost a week past her due date, the day before Midsummer, two days before the scheduled induction, when, one morning, Jo begins cleaning the house.

She starts with her desk. She won't use it, she assumes, for the first weeks once the baby is here. She might as well leave it organized.

After rearranging the living room—moving all the breakables onto hard-to-reach shelves, packing away all the heavy objects that could fall—she starts on the closets. They never fully unpacked from the move into the house more than a year ago. There are still boxes of mementos to find places for.

She pulls down a box of old college notebooks. There are her notes from lit classes. There are her poems from workshops. They are in her handwriting, but they are so unfamiliar, so far away, as if they were written by another person entirely. But, looking more closely, she can see the seeds of her new work within those old poems, the way the thoughts and images have grown over time, turning solidly into themselves.

In the bottom of the packing box, she finds a shoebox and opens it. Inside is a single cone. Sequoia. She is sure it is the cone that Ness rolled into her painting, all those years ago. She knows the shape of it. The way those woody eyes seem to stare, seeing something inside her, something strange and secret.

When she lifts the cone from the box, there is a fall of seeds and a drift of grayblack resindust that looks like ashes. When she turns the cone over in her hand, more seeds scatter.

That's when she feels the muscles move in the depths of her.

That night, as the season shifts to solstice, Liam drives her to the hospital. They move under streetlights on empty roads, skirting the edges of summer. Liam drives quickly but steadily, never exceeding the speed limit, always stopping at the red lights even when no other cars are visible. Beside him, Jo tries to catch her breath between contractions, tries not to think of them when they are not happening, tries to use the breathing she was taught in the birthing class, tries not to dread the next one or the way, she knows, they will get so much worse. She tries to focus, instead, on the way the trees arc over the road, leaves caught in the lights of the street, the way they reach across the glow and shadow.

They drive up the winding road to the hospital. It is so familiar, now, the route. Jo can see it clearly, even in the dark. She steels herself before they lean into every uphill turn.

She begins reviewing her birth plan as they drive. Her doctor told her to write it all out, telling her births never go as planned but it helps to know how you want to make decisions in the moment.

"I want to wait as long as I can for the epidural," Jo reminds Liam. "But I know I'll want to get one at some point."

Liam nods, eyes on the road. Jo winces as her insides tangle with too much solidity, so much more certain than she is.

"And if the doctors recommend a c-section, we do it. I don't want to try to push through it. I just want to do what they say."

"Alright."

"And remember, you want to cut the umbilical cord if you can. They'll probably ask you, but be sure to let them know that when it's time."

"Right. I know."

"And if things go really wrong and there's a choice to be made—"

She winces again, and she isn't sure who interrupts her, Liam or the baby trying to escape her.

"That's not going to happen," Liam says.

"I know that. But if it does."

"Jo, I don't want to talk this way right now."

"But we haven't talked about it. Just listen."

He doesn't say anything.

"It won't be your choice to make. I've made it already. I wrote it down. I choose the baby. Make sure they know that if they need to."

Liam's laugh is edged with fear. He raises his voice a bit when he speaks, as if he is saying the words to the baby, as if he is trying to be heard through her skin. "So dramatic. Always the worst-case scenario with this one. Gotta watch out for that."

"The worst case would be if it happened, and you blamed yourself," Jo mumbles. "This way, you won't have to."

Liam turns the car into the hospital parking lot.

"Do you want me to drop you at the entrance, or do want to walk together?" he asks.

"I think walking would be good," she says. She's been shifting in the seat for the last five minutes, craving movement.

"Alright. I'll park close."

Liam dashes around the car as soon as he pulls the parking break, opening her door before she has collected herself. He grabs the hospital bag from the backseat where the new car seat waits to hold the creature who is twisting inside her. They walk together, holding hands. The trees reach all around them, casting leafy shadows across their bodies.

Part Four

Melt

1

Birth is falling out of time. A gap in the world, yawning wide, lingering forever in fragments.

She throws up. Is throwing up. Knows she has thrown up. She cannot seem to feel it.

Feeling Liam's hands holding back her hair.

Pain against the back. Taking her over. Trapping her inside it.

Inside it, they are telling her she has run through a whole box of vomit bags. She cannot remember.

Remember. How dark the room in the night. Lights kept dim. Just enough to see.

Dimly thinking, once or many times, how the birthing class told her the wildness would take her. When will she go instinctive? When will her mind stop parsing it, analyzing it, counting down hours and centimeters?

Back labor, the nurses whisper to each other, turning her, counting her, moving her this way and that, trying to get the baby to turn too.

People have done this for centuries. She thinks this should reassure her. She feels only the horror of knowledge turn in her mind. People have done *this*, people do *this*, forever, all the time.

The time when the pain moves to the front, becoming less but worse. No longer harrowing against the woody back, soft and fleshy, the pain unbinds itself. She cannot find its edges.

Tight-rope walking balance across this birthdeath edge, the weaving of the room pulls thin as they move through impossible space.

The doctor, not hers, the night doctor, weaving between nurses, muttering about slow progression, about baby heartrate. The unnerving of the bedside manner smile when the doctor explains they will monitor and wait.

They monitor the pain that returns to her back, contained within the trunk of her, pushing into bonebark, fire-filled. It is adjacent to relief, the way she can locate it clearly, the place where the pain ends and her self begins. But the nurses worry.

The pain ends with the needle in the back. Tracing the spine, pushing in, reminders to stay still, perfectly, impossibly still. Pause when the contraction comes. Start again and finish just before the next.

They let her sleep. She does not dream. She stays perfectly, impossibly still.

Surprise at the light of the sunrise, as if she has never seen it, as if, in the depths of the night, she had forgotten the brightness it made. The tenor of the world is changed. The glow of the trees out the window, the way they sing to her, waking her into a dream.

Slownight turn to quickdawn. The rush of the doctor and nurses. Her doctor now, the one she knows. The quick check of numbers. Smiles of relief. The doctor describing how to push. Liam beside her, hand on her shoulder. The light of leafglow. And she knows she is strong enough to do it.
    The baby is a rooted thing,
        bulb pulled from soil,
shelter seeking in the shadow of her chest,
        resting in the rhythm of twoness,
the blood that moved between them.
        She holds them in the quiet shadowbright.
They blink at her.
        Their eyes are the deepest,
all waterwood blue.

2

They don't notice the hands at first, the little film of webbing between the middle and index fingers on both. When the doctor points it out, she doesn't seem concerned.

"We'll make you an appointment with the specialist. It looks pretty simple from what I can see. They'll do x-rays to make sure but if it's what I think it is, it's an easy surgery to release the fingers, just a little skin graft. Usually at a year old. Plenty of time."

"Are there any…complications we should watch for?" Liam asks, flustered and suddenly worried.

Jo is holding the baby's hands, looking down at the places where the fingers connect, wondering at the beauty of them.

The doctor shakes her head. "Not really. It's generally genetic but doesn't usually signify any other issues. Anyone in your family have webbed fingers or toes?"

"No," Liam says. "Not that I know of."

"Selkie hands," Jo murmurs.

Liam's eyes shift from the baby to the doctor and back and forth again, at sea and seeking something solid. The doctor smiles at her indulgently.

After the doctor leaves, Liam examines the baby's hands, murmuring, "How did I not see them?"

"Ness," Jo tells him.

"What?"

"Ness has them. The webbed fingers. They run in her family."

Liam's eyes widen, but he doesn't say anything. Jo cannot read his expression. She cannot tell whether he is looking at her holding the child with pain or love or wonder.

3

Sleep comes in handfuls of minutes, snatched between nursing and rocking and pacing and singing the tiny crying creature to quiet. She is terrified by their helplessness, by her own awkwardness when she tries to hold them in the right positions at her breast. The nurses showed her how, but she cannot seem to repeat it.

"You have a clumsy mother," she whispers to the child as they wail at her for the milk she cannot yet make. "I'll get better, though. I promise."

If she could only sleep, she thinks, she could be strong enough. If she could only have a day or two for the worst of the bleeding to stop, for the memory of the pain and the sharp of its remnants to subside, if she could just have a moment to find herself in this strange leaking space of what is supposed to be her body. Then she could do it. Then she could be a good mother. Calm and wise and strong.

But she will not have those things. This is when she understands the impossible challenge of it, the having to do the hardest part at her weakest point. She knows she will do it, impossible as it is, because she must. But it is so cruel, the ways of bodies. She can feel it in the desperate wails of the baby she holds in her arms, the needy cries that move through them both.

4

In the dim of the early morning, she paces with the child while Liam sleeps on the cot in the corner of the room. The child is not sleeping. They are quiet as they stare up at her with uncanny eyes and she wonders what they see with those blurs of new infant vision. When she looks at them, she thinks they are both very old and very young, both human and something more. There is an elemental sense in them, currentbeat and rootreach, two pools of midnightdeep. Behind their brow, the murmuring of waterleaves.

5

They choose the name the morning they leave the hospital. They want to be sure it is the right one. The administrator tasked with filing the forms comes back three times to check and every time Jo and Liam say, "Not yet."

The knowing comes so suddenly, they question it at first. Are they really so sure? Are they just tired? Rushing? Pressured to decide? But the baby looks at them when they say the word and Jo sees in those eyes they have already claimed it as theirs.

6

Home. A blur of daynight. A mind crowded with the contents of instructional videos detailing advice on nursing, diaper changing, sleep training. Mixing up with the embodied wonders of the tiny hands and feet, the little suckling mouth, the loud of the cries. The fierce currents of the creature. The helpless waves of them. This riverine child.

7

Liam does what he can. He changes the diapers. He wakes with the baby. He paces through the night with the crying. But Jo will not let him try the bottle even after they bring the baby home. No formula. No pumped milk yet. She has read it will inhibit her production this early on. She is determined. She has only nine more weeks. Already, she worries her milk is too low.

8

Jo notices it from the beginning, the way the world seems to lean toward their River. On their first family walk, they all blink at the bright of the day.

"What time is it?" Liam asks as he pushes the baby carriage. His face is drawn with exhaustion, but he is smiling, a fatherly warmth glowing out of him.

"I have no idea," Jo says.

A flicker lands on the hood of the carriage, perches for a moment, head tilting curiously, before alighting.

"That's a strangely tame bird," Liam says.

Later that week, when Jo sits in the backyard with the child, a hummingbird pauses right next to them, wings abuzz and treading the air, for a full minute. Beneath the sequoia, a cone drops like a gift, or a point being made.

Jo thinks of Ness, the pull of her, the way the cats and crows would follow. The child gazes out at the world with their eyes that are bluer than blue, pulling it closer.

9

That summer, they are warned of the heat to come, and so they plan for it. They hang heavy blankets across the sunny windows to block the warming light. They watch the temperature inside the house creep upward. They turn the air conditioner as high as it will go. By midmorning, the temperature rises well past the usual summer afternoon high. They shut the doors of all the unessential rooms, abandoning them to heat.

River, only eight weeks old, won't stop crying. The baby, she is sure, can sense something is wrong.

They will be fine, Jo tells herself, as long as the old air conditioner keeps working. They will be uncomfortable, but fine. She worries about the air conditioner. It was only meant for their small old apartment, bought second hand and already worn, the cheapest one they could find at the time, and the smallest. She worries about the power too. The grid is not made for the whole city to run air conditioning full blast for days. When they first moved up here after college, no one had air conditioners. Even a few years ago, any more than a handful of truly hot summer days felt impossible.

Now, outside, the temperature is rising to 110 degrees Fahrenheit. Inside, it is still only 86.

On the first day of the heat, the inside temperature reaches almost to 90 and stays above 80 through the depths of the night.

10

That night, Jo cannot sleep, even as the baby does. She lays in bed next to Liam, quiet as she scrolls through the news on her phone. They are trapped beneath a dome of heat. A curious anomaly of air currents and temperature that makes a bubble over the region. Record highs. Record hospitalizations for heat stroke. They are already counting the deaths. There shouldn't be this many, Jo keeps thinking as she reads the stories about people found alone in their homes with broken air conditioners or no cooling at all, people found at bus shelters and parks, within tents, beneath bridges with no one there to help them.

The heat can creep up on you, one article quotes from a doctor. *You often don't know when you've crossed into the threshold of danger.*

One more day, Jo thinks. The weather predicts that the heat will break the next night.

11

On the second day, Jo rocks River and draws the curtain back to peer out the window. The bright of the sun makes her squint. At first, the yard looks desolate, still and heat-emptied. Then, she sees the crow. The bird is standing, beak open, on the ground beneath the sequoia, right next to the dish of water she put out for the animals that morning. The bird looks askew. Jo keeps watching, humming softly to the baby so close to sleep in her arms, waiting for the bird's beak to close. They are swaying back and forth, ruffled feathers sticking out at strange angles. Their beak does not close. Jo finally understands what she is seeing. The crow is panting. She has never seen such a thing before. Not in any weather. Always, the crows seem so solid. The strongest of birds.

She watches a moment more. The crow does not move from beneath the tree. The crow does not stop panting.

12

Later, the baby napping in their crib while Liam waters the vegetable garden in the front yard for the third time that morning, Jo ventures outside with a handful of ice cubes for the water dish beneath the tree. The heat is like nothing she has ever felt before. It is suffocating. There is no time between the stepping outside and the feeling of burning that comes over her. She cannot breathe the air. She feels a rising panic.

Jo approaches the crow slowly, cautious. The bird is afraid, and she fears for them. They are still panting when they try to fly up to the lowest branches of the sequoia to escape her. The bird's wings crumple and flail as they miss the intended perch and topple back to ground. Jo hears the pained cry and thinks, at first, it comes out of the bird or the tree. Then she realizes it has come from her own throat.

The ice cubes melting in her hands, she considers, momentarily, whether she might take the crow inside with her. Maybe she could throw a blanket over them and bundle them into the relative cool of the house.

The crow eyes her, terrified. She imagines it, the way the scared creature, trapped inside, would batter against the windows and walls, desperate for escape. That's if she could catch them at all. She wishes she could speak to the crow. She wishes they would understand her if she did. She wishes they could tell her how to help. She is useless in a lack of language.

The ice slides into the water dish quickly, and she hopes she hasn't scared the crow away from it. She retreats back through the door to the house.

The sobs move through her before she feels the cool of inside air. She stands by the closed door and weeps for the bird she does not know how to save, for the baby she has born into a time of panting panicked crows that can no longer fly.

13

In the living room, she finds Liam on the couch looking shaken. She sits next to him, puts a hand on his. He jerks away. His hands are trembling.

"It isn't supposed to be like this," he whispers, careful not to wake River in the next room. His whisper sounds like a hiss, pitched too high, a kettle brought to boil. "This is all wrong."

"I know."

"The garden is dying. The tomatoes can't handle this, however much I water them. Look at the rhododendron leaves. They're burning."

"I know."

"We're fielding constant phone calls about the neighborhood gardens, but I don't know what to tell anyone beyond water and shade. I don't know how to save them. And what if our air conditioner breaks? Our unit isn't meant for a house. I should have replaced it. What if the power goes out? I knew I should have bought one of those battery generators. Why didn't I do that? What was I thinking? We have a baby, and we aren't prepared."

Jo feels an unusual calm come over her in the face of his worry. They are inside the thing she has feared. The crisis is descending upon them. But they are managing. They are keeping their baby safe. They are doing their best for the crows.

"The heat is supposed to break tonight," she reminds him. "We're almost through it. After, we'll buy a new air conditioner. We'll save up for that generator. We'll be better prepared."

Liam groans, but he doesn't pull away this time when she takes his hand.

14

The heat breaks that evening. In a matter of hours, it falls by more than thirty degrees. They throw open the windows. When Jo steps outside, after putting River down for the night, she cannot believe how different the air feels from earlier that afternoon. A cool breeze moves under the pink of the dusky sky. She can hear the birds again. They sing. She looks, at first, for bodies on the ground. She fears she will find a pile of feathers, dark and shadowy, by the water dish. But she doesn't. Instead, she sees a squirrel run across the lawn. The neighbor's cat moves under the bushes. She can hear Liam watering the garden in the front of the house again, trying to revive the plants.

She lays on her back in the cool grass and looks up, exhausted, into the bluegreen branches of the sequoia. She feels the tree's roots webbing through the ground beneath her, holding her up. The earth against her back is solid and certain. The breeze moves across her face.

She watches the crows wheeling overhead, looping with the currents of the wind, borne up by the air. One dips and lands on the sequoia's lower branches, cawing.

Jo sits up. She is sure this is the crow from afternoon. She is sure they have come down to speak to her.

"You're okay," she says.

The crow caws again and takes flight, circling up into the evening, flapping their strong wings.

Laying back on the grass, Jo feels the tears slide sideways down her cheeks, eddying to the thirsty ground.

15

The tiny bodies are everywhere she walks. All that next week, taking the baby out in the front pack, she sees, at the edges of sidewalks and trails, many little deaths. Fledglings fallen to heat. They are so small, curled up beneath the trees that hold the nests they dove from.

She reads that this is a common response to intense heatwaves. Their nests grown too warm, the fledglings try to escape and fall, not yet ready to fly.

When she sees them, she does not stop to look. She passes by quickly, holding her own baby closer.

For days after, when she hears the birds singing, she wonders if they are crying in grief.

16

Ten weeks after the birth, the night before Jo is set to return to work, River sleeps for a full six hours for the first time. Jo does not. She thinks she will go to her desk. She has been longing for it. The solitude of it. The quiet where her poems might whisper themselves into being. She has hardly written since the birth. The weeks have rippled by so quickly, leaving her in the wake of half-thoughts, fragments of fragments of lines, nothing cohered or coherent.

Now, the desk has become a stranger's land. A place she remembers but can no longer claim. She has been away for too long.

Instead, she pulls the notebook with her poems from the drawer and takes it outside. The night is warm and dark. She brings a flashlight and a pen.

At first, she convinces herself that she is only reading it. She is picking up where she left off, reminding herself that she can write a poem, a whole notebook's worth of them. But, when she reaches the second poem, she knows something is wrong. A clang in the brain. A forced line. A blank space left dead on the page. She thought she had finished them. She thought each poem was complete, a small word world to itself. At first, the despair of it. Then, the possibilities.

Outside, beneath the sequoia, she pulls the poems apart, tearing page after page from the notebook and spreading them across the tree's roots. She doesn't read them so much as she hears them. They whisper up at her from the pages. Ink twists over roots, papers rustle across needles, and she can feel how the poems should be together.

By morning, she will not be sure who finished them, who scratched out the last revised lines, who ordered the pages—herself or the sequoia, or some conversation between them. She will only know that they are fundamentally altered. The poems have been transformed into something beyond their individual poetry. They have grown into an intertwining system.

17

She doesn't touch her writing again for months.

The time blurs into drop offs and pick ups and bedtimes and waking, always, too early, too often, and missing, always, too much.

At work Jo is constantly leaving her desk to pump. They set up a chair for her in the shower room in the basement where the bikes are stored. They have no lactation room in the building, and this is better than the stalls in the public restroom. The company has never needed a lactation room before. She is the first in their ten years running to give birth while employed.

The shower room is windowless and musty and without internet. She feels, every few hours, like she is descending into the earth, making her baby's milk in the caverns beneath the world to bring it back up to the anesthetized light of the office fridge. It is dark and private in that world beneath the world, where she imagines the roots of trees pushing up against foundations, the rhythms of the pump echoing the rhythms of water pulled from soil. It is in emergence that Jo loses a sense of her shape. She is mortified every time, setting her clear plastic bottles next to everyone's sack lunches. She brings a lunch pail just to hide the bottles in. But everyone knows what is inside, knows where she is going when she leaves the office thrice a day with her pump and all its tubing trying to hide in a tote bag.

She worries she will go down to the basement one day and find the milk has ceased. Already, it seems so small, the tiny accumulated drops collecting in the bottom of the bottles. Already, it takes so long to collect them. Technically, she is permitted twenty-minute lactation breaks two times per workday in addition to her lunch break. But no one says anything when she takes an extra ten minutes or leaves the office more frequently. She tries to be frequent. But the office meetings pile up and many days she finds, by noon, her breasts aching and hard, that she has not left the office once. She thinks, on these days, that, when she pumps, the milk will fill the jar. But it never does. It is always the same, that finger's width of yellowwhite.

18

Jo begins collecting fallen walnuts that first autumn. She doesn't take the green ones. She looks for the ones that are sinking into shadow.

Pushing the carriage along the path in the park, she veers beneath the tall walnut tree, startling the squirrels and crows at their breakfasts. She sings to River as she scans the ground, swoops down to take the husks she needs, and stores them in the bottom compartment of the carriage.

Back home, she puts them in a box in the garage to molder. She'll wait until they turn completely dark, all their green gone. Then she'll tear them open for the ink.

She wants to make it herself, so she looks it up online. She thinks that it might help the writing. A kind of magic spell. Summoning words with tree fruit and stained fingers.

There is so much to write. The words move through her, but she can't catch them quickly enough. Not with River in her arms on the couch, needing one hand to hold them and one hand to balance. Not with the office days filling up with pumping tubes and too many assignments, always too much squeezed between meetings and trips underground. Sometimes, in the basement, she manages a line or two scrawled in a notebook. Or, nursing River, she'll reach for her phone and type snatches of phrases with her thumb, promising herself that she'll come back to them later. But then, in the tangle of milk and diapers and crying and sleeping and waking every few hours, she forgets. Or, when she comes back to them, she finds that she cannot fit the lines together again, can no longer remember what she intended her jumbles of words to become.

The ink will take time. At least a month to cure once the husks have gone fully dark. Then she'll strain it and boil it down. Only then will it be ready.

19

Sometimes, in the middle of the night, River at her breast seeking more milk than she can make, before Jo gives up to heat the formula, she slips into a space running parallel to waking. Not quite a dream. But not quite not a dream. In that space, the child changes. Fur and fangs currenting. The suckling sounds become the sighs of hungry roots digging earthward. The cries are caws. The flutter of wings and leaves in the air between them. The baby soft as moss, insistent as stone. The childcubkitten. The filamental weave of them.

Always, the notdream will pass. She will fall out of the parallel stream and back into the familiar. The child in her arms. Frustrated and seeking.

Then unlatch. Then holding with one hand and, one-handed, scooping and heating the formula. Then feeding the child. Drinking it all down so fast. Then rocking to sleep. And down in the crib with the hand on the back, the stroking of hair, the kiss goodnight. And back to bed herself. The burrowing under the blankets. The remnants of notdreams diving into the dreams themselves, becoming something new.

Later, when she opens her eyes, they will tangle, the dreams and notdreams shuffling into nearwaking. In that moment of merged space, she thinks, sometimes, she can see the reality of this mothering. She thinks, sometimes, she can find its full shape.

20

When the walnut husks have lost their last green, she mashes them with a rock. They come apart more easily than she expected. She pulls them open, prying out the walnuts with their hard shells, and leaves those hearts in the yard for the squirrels. It is only the husks that she needs, the black of them.

She puts them in a large jar and pours the water over. A spoonful of vinegar to keep the mold away. She stirs it up, covers the jar, and puts it in the back of the garage, away from the light. The ink of the husks will seep into the water, slow, steady, sure. She will wait. She marks her calendar for one month in the future. She won't open the jar until then.

21

Dropping off at daycare, always, someone is nursing. In the daycare fridge, always the full bottles of milk left to sustain the babies through the day. Jo wonders how the others make so much. She dutifully hands her meager supply over every morning with the same instructions. Use this first. Her box of powdered formula sits on the shelf above the sink. It isn't the only one, but she always suspects it is used most frequently.

Each day, before she leaves for work, she sits with River on a cushion in the corner and dutifully pulls up her shirt, unlatches her nursing bra, wishing she could do it unembarrassed like the others, wishing it felt simpler. Across from her, always, someone else in mirror image, but calmer, surer. The baby settling at the breast contentedly. Not like River, kneading and pulling and fussing and looking up at her, eyes filled with the confusion of betrayal, struggling for milk.

She tells herself it is better this way. It will leave her freer sooner. When the nursing is done, her body will no longer be relied upon for sustenance. She and River can build a different kind of bond. One outside of that fraught feeding. And it is better for Liam too. He can make up the formula and have that time with River. It will be better. It will be fine. Her baby is fed. The ways of it don't matter. She believes that.

But, every morning, the ease of the others, the ways they will sometimes talk amongst themselves of storing freezers

238

full of goldwhite baggies, the plenty of the bottles they set on the shelves of the fridge, make her feel like a shrunken thing.

She imagines, sometimes, as she sits on her cushion with River, that day when the milk will cease to come. The sad relief of it. It will be over then. She will be done with it. They will sit together on this cushion and find there is nothing left. River will wail and she will smile. Selfish and horrible, dried up amidst the milk of others.

22

It is cold when she collects the jar from the corner of the garage. The glass looks like it holds the depths of midnight liquified inside it. But when she opens it and dips a stick in and draws it across a piece of paper, the liquid is so light. A bright auburn. Is it strong enough, she wonders, to pin words to the page and keep them there? Has she done it wrong? Perhaps it only needs more time. She closes the lid and marks her calendar for another month.

23

Each time River latches, she prepares herself for it to be the last. Each time grows shorter and shorter. Each time, she has to add more formula to the bottle.

She tells herself she has done her best. She wants to believe it. Six months is good. Six months is something.

She stops pumping at work. She is only managing the smallest thread of milk now, hardly enough to cover the bottoms of the bottles. She packs the tubes away. She hides the chords and the pump. She doesn't want to look at them.

Jo thinks the weaning will happen organically, that it will be River who decides. She thinks she won't be the one to start it. But, every night, the crying, the rocking away all the little bubbles of swallowed air that come when the milk won't. River is determined. River isn't giving up. So, in the end, Jo has to.

She chooses the time. Morning. She has some milk then. It is always calm and close and sleepy. River with their eyes still filmed with dreams, looking up at her with blue. She tells them it is the last time. They won't understand, but she wants them to know, somewhere beyond the language of the thing, the severing of it, the way they will have to grow toward each other differently. She doesn't want them to be surprised.

But they are surprised, when, after daycare, there is no nursing on the couch before dinner, when, after dinner, even after the full bottle of formula, they reach for her breast and are denied. She cuddles River close, smiles sadly, and shakes her head. They reach again. She holds them closer as they pound with their tiny fists, angry now and wailing. She holds them until she leaks two drops of milk onto her shirt. Then the holding itself seems like cruelty. She hands River to Liam and locks herself in the bathroom.

Cold and brittle, she sits on the side of the tub and covers her ears. She tries to take deep breaths. She tells herself that River will forgive her this, won't even remember it. She will be the one to remember.

The laugh escapes her suddenly, a deep hollowing sound echoing from an empty space inside her, bouncing off the shiny tiled surface of the floor. She can't stop it. It floods out of her, winging its way to Liam who shouts to her through the door and the laughter and the wailing child, asking if she is ok.

She sinks all the way down to the floor, damp shirted, still laughing.

"I'll be out in a minute," she shouts back, hoping he understands the voice that doesn't sound like hers, that comes out wild and sharp, a notdream creature, barking over, growing thorns.

By the time she leaves the bathroom she has changed her shirt and collected her humanmother face again. She takes the wailing River and holds them close and smiles reassurance at the worried husband. She wonders if he sees, the something else that is moving behind the womanface, stalking through the dark inside her eyes.

24

By the time the ink is ready, fall is turning into winter. The husks have cured for almost a whole season. But the ink is darker now. Deeper.

She strains it with cheesecloth and pours the liquid into a saucepan on the stove. Boiling is meant to concentrate it and give it a richer hue. And the boiling will keep the mold away, for a while.

On the stove, the ink smells old and wild. The bubbles brighten over the dark surface. The steam rises, curls around the air, making its own shapes.

Walnut tree grows the husks slow
    springs them to fall on the grass
        gathering squirrels and crows and human hands.
Roots span beneath
    draw together the unseen world
        a simmer in the pot, ink to charm the words
            to hold them.

The next night, she fills her pen. She hovers it over the page, nervous. The first words cannot be wrong. She cannot waste the work of the walnut tree or the husks or the jar or the pot or her own hands that still hold the stains of it.

The sound of the simmering still echoes inside her, the smell of the ink on the stove still caught in her nose. She starts

there, circles outward, moves words around the tree itself.
The ink holds a rhythm inside it, a quiet pulsing she can
follow if she listens. Her own rhythms shift to meet it.
   beat of sunleafbreath
   movement of moonwaterblood
   branchroot through woodypage
   inkseep to the edges

the letters

The poems of this ink are new—hers and not hers, human
and tree twining to something else entirely.

25

It is early spring, and River has begun to walk when they go for the family hike through the forest half an hour's drive from the city. Liam carries the child in a pack, but Jo can tell River is restless, longing to put feet on ground to practice propelling their small body forward. Jo points out the trillium blossoming in the still chilly sun, three leaves and three petals. White as melting snow. Purple as twilight.

"Three like us," Liam says. "Mom, Dad, and River."

They stop on the banks of a stream for lunch. While Liam sets up a picnic, Jo takes River's shoes and socks off, rolls up the cuffs of their pants for wading. The air is cool but warming with the springtime afternoon. The water will be cold. Jo takes off her own shoes and socks, steps into the stream holding River's hand, letting them decide when to dip a toe in. She thinks they will hesitate, put one foot in and then take it out again. She thinks they may decide not to wade in at all, worried by the rocky, muddy floor or the way the water glints by in steady sun-streaked ripples. But she is wrong. River walks right in, wades deeper, all the way to the middle of the stream almost before she has realized it. She follows, holding their hand, surprised by how her child seems to walk better, more assuredly, in water than on land. River looks up at her, laughing, and stomps their feet up and down, sending up a glittering spray. She laughs and stomps too, wiggling cold toes through the rocky mud.

245

On the shore, Liam calls, "Be careful. Don't fall in."

He keeps his tone light, but Jo can hear the anxiety beneath it, the way he is unsure whether or not to be nervous. River is really stomping now and, though she is holding tightly to their hand, she thinks the falling in is imminent. But the stream is shallow, and she has thought ahead to bring an extra set of clothes. Disaster is unlikely. She smiles reassurance back at Liam, the look she has discovered in their parenthood to tell him she has planned ahead, that all is well and safe and comfortable. She thinks of it as the mother look because she learned it from her own, who learned it, no doubt, from her own, and all the way down the matrilineal line it has travelled, this mask of certainty she has now accustomed herself to put on when it is needed. Liam sees the look and relaxes, leans against the trunk of a tree and tilts his head up toward the sun.

In the stream, Jo hears the splash of the fall before she sees it. It happens in the moment when Liam is not watching them. The slip and the change. The change is momentary. It happens in between the tug on her arm and the realization that River has fallen into the water. It happens just before Liam looks back at them to see her pick River up to carry them to shore. But in her memory, the moment will lengthen, expanding to hold the whole day, seeping into other moments, silvering the afters and befores.

The water only comes to River's chest when they fall, so the vision Jo sees is blurred in streaks of reflecting liquid sun. Beneath the water, perhaps, a sheen of silver, covering over River's feet and ankles, glinting gray beneath the light that flecks through waves. A glimmer at the hands, connected at the middle fingers, webbed and catching at the streambed. And above the water, that subtle tinge of green, hair rustling.

Their eyes, when they look at her, have darkened. They are something between dusky sylvan shadows and the uncanny blue of deep sea.

Jo looks down at a child who is other than a child—a wooded thing, forestwatercreature. She pulls them from the stream and, by the time she has walked them back to shore, the moment has passed. She looks but cannot see it anymore, the silver and the green, the fur and leaves. There is only River now, her mostly human child.

Liam is beside them, making jokes about falling while unpacking the dry clothes, lightening the mood. Soon, River will laugh as their parents peel off their soaking clothes. But now, they look up at Jo, eyes still halfway to waterwoods.

26

When River is almost one, they have the consult with the surgeon. Jo holds the child while the doctor looks at their hands, gently spreads the fingers and smiles at the webs between them.

"This is an easy one," the doctor tells them. "Just the skin. We'll cut a zigzag to avoid any stiffness in the future. We'll take the graft from the inside elbow. Once it's healed, you'll hardly even notice it."

Jo tries not to imagine it, the cuts to be made between the fingers, the way the skin will seep with the deep red of their blood. They haven't talked about the question of not doing the surgery. So, Jo asks if that would be a possibility.

"Well, it'll impede the movement of the hands. You'd have to adapt things for them. Could make instruments difficult, but people manage it just fine. So, that's an option. Most parents choose the surgery. But you don't have to."

In the car, as Jo buckles River into the car seat, Liam is concerned.

"We're doing the surgery," he says. "Right? We aren't really considering not doing it?"

"Of course," Jo says. "I just want to be sure we know all the options."

"Because I really think this is the right thing to do. Any other option makes it much harder on River later than it has to be."

"I know."

Jo snaps the car seat buckle together, and River reaches out to grab a strand of her hair, grasping it with all their fingers, the two middle ones joined together, moving as one. Jo wonders if those fingers will still move in parallel after the surgery, holding that memory of connection. She wonders if, after, the fingers will always feel the loss, the strangeness of the space made between them.

27

In the weeks leading up to the surgery, far to the south, the wildfires move through old sequoia groves. Scrolling through articles, Jo recognizes the place, the parking lot, the campsite, the trees. It is the same place where she and Liam hiked and camped, before the child, those many years ago.

In the pictures accompanying the reports, firefighters wrap a few of the older sequoias in what looks like aluminum foil. The articles explain this as an attempt at fireproofing. The material glistens, startling metallic on the woody redbrown bark of the giant trees. It is so small, this silver sheeting, set against the large of their trunks. Jo wonders if the efforts will be futile. The trees are giants. The wildfires something even larger. The humans seem to move on such a tiny scale before these elementals.

The crews can't wrap the whole forest. They choose the oldest and the largest trees. Jo tries to imagine it. The horror of the choosing. These, we will try to save. These, we will let the flames take.

She can see the way the flames, when they come to the grove, will glint off the silver, trying to lick up the trunks. No one really seems to know what will happen. These fires are different than the ones the trees were made to withstand. They are hotter, larger. These are highway jumping fires, town decimating fires, fires that eat up ancient flame-scarred groves in moments.

It will be the young ones, she realizes, unprotected, not yet hardened to maturity, that will go first. The children of the old will fall before them.

28

It has been almost a year since she dreamed of Ness. She thought, after the birth, that the dreams were finished, that all of it was finished, that she wouldn't see Ness again, waking or sleeping. But this night, the dreams come back to her.

In the first dream, she sees Ness painting an image of hands. In the picture, the hands cup water between them. The glint of the liquid makes it seem, at first, like the hands are holding light. Beneath Ness's brush, the hands shift, grow together. The fingers merge. They grow claws that curve around the water, sharp and delicate.

When Jo looks at Ness's hand that holds the paintbrush, it no longer seems like a hand at all. It has become a web of silver threads glinting.

29

Every night, after River goes to sleep, Jo pulls out her computer and searches, again, for Ness. She hasn't looked since the pregnancy. Now, almost a year after the birth, she wishes she could ask Ness what to do. Ness had the surgery at close to River's age. She never expressed any regret about that. But then, Jo never thought to ask before.

She wonders what Ness's life would be if her parents had left her fingers as she had been born with them. Would she have been able to paint in the same ways? Would she have wished her parents had chosen differently? Perhaps she would have chosen the surgery herself, later, when she had that choice. Would she have resented her parents for placing the burden of the decision on her? For not doing the hard and bloody thing themselves?

Jo knows what the right thing to do is. She knows it in that way she seems to know things now, sometimes, about her child, about what they will need for the future. River will need the full freedom of their hands. She knows this. She doesn't know why or how. She just knows. Like she knows the surgery will go well. Like she knows the child will thrive. She knows what River needs. She just wants more certainty. She wants someone else to tell her what she knows to be true will be true.

And behind all that, another kind of knowing. This surgery, this cutting apart of webbed fingers, is a human thing to do, is a kind of claiming, she worries, for one kind of reality. What if she breaks something essential inside of her child? Like stealing a skin.

30

"Boy or girl?" the well-meaning woman asks in the park as they pass by, River napping in the carriage. It is a common enough question, often the first they encounter in public spaces. Jo is used to deflecting it, usually by a deft change of subject. But on this day, she is distracted. She doesn't answer immediately. She doesn't want to have to manage the moment and navigate the stranger out of it.

The woman is smiling, the enchanted smile of a grown up encountering a child. But, as she waits for the answer, the smile turns expectant, begins to be annoyed by the pause, the way her confusion extends within it.

"Boy or girl?" she repeats, louder this time, nervous, her voice rising into the register of human lost in forest.

Jo smiles the mother smile.

"Selkie," she says as they walk past the woman. She does not look to see the reaction.

31

She watches the routes of the fires move toward the maps of the sequoia groves. She checks her phone throughout the days at work, scanning the headlines, waiting for news.

She wonders, as she walks from the bus stop to pick River up from daycare, whether the sequoias here in her city, all these greenbrown giants sprouting up from backyards and parks, know the plight of their fellows to the south. She wonders if they feel it in their roots, if they can sense it on the wind.

She thinks she can feel them holding tighter to the earth, to this region they have been brought to, shipped north, away from home, and planted with all these human hands for all these human purposes. Perhaps it is a refuge now, wetter than their drought-parched native groves as the climate shifts and the fires change.

She walks beneath them, scrolling on her phone, helpless in her witnessing.

32

Liam is watching the news of the sequoia groves too. At dinner, as River grips tiny spears of potato and halved grapes in their highchair, Liam wonders aloud about how long the sequoias will last.

"You know, people are starting to move them," he says. "All over the world. Intentionally. There's even a logging company trying to relocate the gene pools of whole sequoia groves by planting new ones from the seeds. Apparently, the trees would do it on their own eventually. They have during other climate shifts. But this shift is so fast."

"All of it is so tiny," Jo says. "Wrapping individual trees. Planting seeds. It's not enough."

"Of course not," Liam says. "But it's not nothing."

Later that night, they argue about the surgery. The date has been set, but Jo still hasn't called the hospital back to confirm.

"What is it?" Liam asks. "Why are you hesitating?"

Jo can't find the answer.

"We're so lucky," Liam continues. "It's a simple procedure. Just skin. No bone or muscle involved. No likely complications. Great outcomes. We have health insurance. We can pay for it. We have a great doctor. We can give our child this. We can make things a little easier for them. We can give them the full use of their hands."

257

"What if River comes back different? What if they lose something?"

"I don't understand."

"Like in the stories. What if it's like stealing a part of them? Forcing them into humanness?"

Jo watches a hardening behind her husband's eyes. She can feel the fear coming off of him.

"They are human."

"Maybe."

"Jo."

"I know," she says, knowing how she sounds and frustrated with the limits of language, "I can't explain it to you."

"Try."

She knows it will frighten him. She knows he won't understand. She says it anyway.

"They're human. But they're more than human too. Can't you see it? They're human and they're tree and water and selkie and mycelium and who knows what other things. They're human and they're forest. They're human and they're river."

"This isn't poetry. This is our child's life."

"Those are the same thing."

"Jo, please, just think practically. The decision we make will have real ramifications in the real world for our real child."

"I know that."

"I don't know what to do when you get like this."

"Just give me time. Just let me work it through."

Liam throws up his hands. It looks, for a moment, like he might burst into tears.

"We aren't that different," Jo tells him, trying to be reassuring. "We want what's best for River. We usually agree on what that is. We usually come to the same conclusions. We just get there differently. Just give me time to get there with you. In my own way."

She speaks with more certainty than she feels. She worries, when she follows the thread to its end, it will set her down in some other place than with her husband, than as the human mother doing what is best for her human child.

33

The second time she dreams of Ness, she sees River with her. Ness is dressing them in fur, pulling the silver skin over their arms and legs, fastening endless buttons.

"What are you doing?" Jo asks.

"Taking them home," Ness tells her.

"Where?"

Ness points out to the horizon, flat and dark and impossibly far. Jo feels the ache of distance in her bones.

"Wait," she says.

Ness is pulling the fur up and over River's head, disappearing the child within.

Last, the hands. First, Jo thinks they are covered in gloves. Then she sees the claws.

"Wait."

But Ness can't hear her anymore. The dream dissolves into a blur of fur and claws and water. And River's eyes, gone dark and seal-like. Not knowing her when they look back.

34

Three days before the surgery, Liam is outside picking vegetables with River, pulling the green beans from the long vines they planted together that spring. Jo is sitting under the sequoia, watching. They are a pair, father and child, gardening together. River mirrors Liam's movements, gentle and precise, grasping each bean as if the plant could feel their touch.

River runs to her, climbs onto her lap and burrows their head in the soft of her shoulder. She wraps her arms around them, sinking into the animal warmth they make together. She leans back against the tree's vast trunk, holding the weight of her child, and closes her eyes.

Behind her lids, the scatter of seeds. The dry heat that melts resin, opens cones. The green that weaves through ash, growing into light, born from decimation. They reach for each other underground and overair, all that green, all those rooted things. They wind around each other into all the seasons of seeding to come.

River scrambles off her lap, intent on something. When she opens her eyes, she sees their small hands wrapped around the sequoia cone they've just plucked from the ground. They hold the cone out to her. The cone seems to blink beneath the child's fingertips, waking up.

"Plant," River tells her.

And so, they plant.

Liam finds the way. How long it takes to dry the cone, to germinate the seeds once they release. How to pot them. How long to wait for sprouts.

In the end, just one will survive. From all the tiny green tendrils, the single sapling in the pot, growing steady, gaining height.

They will put the sapling on the porch shaded by the branches of the larger tree, and there the sapling will remain for years before they find a place to plant them in the ground, freeing their roots to reach into the earth.

35

Jo watches a video of the firefighters pulling the silver from the trees. She can almost feel the crinkle of unwrapping echoing over her own skin. The reports say that the flames came within yards of the sequoias. But there they are, in the after of it. They still stand, scarred with old fire, wrapped in new silver, spanning the skyground.

36

The night before the surgery, Jo writes in the blood of trees, rending words from her slivered sheets of woodflesh. Her paper and pen have never felt so violent.

In the morning, there will be the waking. In the morning, there will be the drive to the hospital. The same hospital where River was born. Up there on the hill in the trees. It feels circular, this return. Just a few days shy of a year.

She wants to believe the choice has been made. That she has already made it. But she can't settle herself to it. She has read and read about the condition. She and Liam have talked and talked. And still, her mind moves circles around it.

To cut the skin is a decision made. There is finality in it.

The year before, the cutting of the umbilical cord, the long journey out from inside her. The final severing. Six months ago, the nursing ended, the dried up milk.

This isn't the same. This is a choice.

To wait would be to leave a pathway open. Delay, perhaps. Or a decision later. Or never. An always possibility.

<pre>
    if   to cut is
                                                       to sever
                               webs
    of moonsun
    of skyground
</pre>

to cut is
to burn

the path back to

waterwilds

to cut is
to claim

to unmagic

to cut is
to make

a scar

root it deep

decimation creating

a leafing

37

In the final dream of Ness, Jo finds her standing by the ocean in the dark, her face turned out to sea.

She thinks, at first, Ness won't see her, thinks that she is invisible in the ways that dreams turn dreamers into bodiless witnesses. So, it surprises her when Ness turns and looks her straight in the eye.

Ness stretches out her hand. At the fingers, the silver threads are glistening, connecting through disconnection, there and not there, webs and open space.

"We hold the between whatever we choose," Ness tells her.

The scars are webs. The webs are scars.

And then the dream goes dark.

Part Five

Margin

1

The sky is just beginning to darken as Jo rides the bus home. That evening, she watches the purplepink of it, the way the blue comes in from above as the orange of the sun disappears behind the city. The buildings glow with reflected light as the forested hills beyond turn to shadow.

The bus moves east, crossing over the river by bridge, heading away from downtown toward the city's rings of residential neighborhoods. Jo settles in for the ride, tracing the memory of the evening.

She's coming from a poetry reading, an open mic hosted by a local literary organization. Open to anyone, everyone. All you had to do was sign up at the door. She didn't sign up. She'd intended to. She'd even brought a poem to read, a recent one, one she felt proud of. But, listening to the other readers, she'd lost her nerve. It wasn't that she thought her poem wasn't good enough. The quality of the readings differed wildly from poet to poet. The amateurs mingling with the established—that was part of the point of it, a democratization of the microphone. Everyone's efforts were applauded, regardless of how far along they were in their craft. It wasn't about the craft of it. She knew her poems could stand up to scrutiny over line and image and meter. It was that, as she listened to all these other poems about love affairs and childhood traumas and wars and medical emergencies and marital disputes, her poems began to feel unfitted. They were filled with shifting leaves and slantlight, overgrown with roots and shadowy spaces that flickered in and out of words. They seemed from another world entirely. She held them in her hands, these attempts to render trees and ferns and crows and ice and air in human syntax, to find language and lines and forms to hold them, to allow them to speak through her. She held her poems in the midst of all those people and felt so not quite human.

She is gazing out at the river, caught in an overpowering sense of aloneness, when she sees it—a flash in the water, a break in the waves. The bus has almost reached the end of the bridge. She can see the riverbank below and the thing that is swimming toward it—too big to be a fish, too graceful for a person. The thing glides, cutting through the current, and pulls itself up onto shore. It shines silvergray in the twilight, a sheen of water sparking over fur. And then, just as the bus is cresting the bridge and turning off it onto the streets, just as the riverbank begins to leave her view, she thinks she sees the change begin—the fur turning to hair, the human arms and legs emerging in a flash of skin.

"Ness," she thinks, as the vision disappears from view, as the other side of the river takes her from the space between sky and water, back to the city streets.

2

When Jo returns home, River is already sleeping. It is quiet and dark in the living room, and she stands for a moment, listening to shadows. Through the doorway to the kitchen, she can see Liam sitting at the table, solid and real in the glow of the overhead lights. She thinks, at first, she will not go to him, that she will slip silent through the dark and into the bedroom and straight into dreaming without disturbing the strangeness of the evening. Later, he will find her there, curled under the covers, lost to him in sleep, caught up in a world he cannot see.

She steps into the kitchen. Liam smiles up at her, warmly human with a smudge of sap across his forehead. Piles of seeds and cones are strewn across the table like treasures being sorted. He has a box beside him and a stack of envelopes. It feels reassuringly domestic, their particular version of domestic: dried lavender hung in the corners of the windows, bulbs waiting in the garage, always a little dirt under the fingernails. She settles back into the familiar rhythms. She almost forgets what she thinks she saw.

"How was the reading?" Liam asks.

"Okay," she tells him. "Did River get down alright?"

Liam laughs. "Do they ever?"

River has taken, at almost three years old, to running around the house after bedtime, babbling about the day.

Every night, getting the child to sleep feels like trying to turn back the tide.

"We should never have switched from the crib," Jo says.

Liam laughs again. "You don't think they'd be climbing out by now?"

He continues his work as they talk, placing handfuls of seeds, a few from each sorted pile, into each stamped envelope, then setting each envelope in the box. It's a familiar pattern. The envelopes will be sent out to planters across the city, becoming vegetables, maybe a few flowers, in the community gardens. They'll go to school clubs and backyard hobbyists and native plant programs.

"But at least it would be some deterrent," Jo says.

"Or maybe more of a challenge. I could see River really enjoying climbing over a crib rail every night."

Jo can see it too, the grin of glee on the child's face, all mischief and pride as they scale the crib wall.

"Our little sprite."

His piles of seeds diminished, Liam brings a small package from under the table, places it gently next to his box of filled envelopes. From the package, he begins to pull out cones, placing two apiece into each still-open envelope. In the glow of the kitchen light, Jo watches each woody eye wink its hints of sap, all green and brown and gray and glistening. Liam handles the cones with care. She can see him imagining the tree each could become as he holds them.

"Sequoia cones?" Jo asks.

Liam nods. "It's something new we're trying. Kind of an experiment. One of our partner organizations sent us these. They're collecting seeds from trees that are struggling in the droughts, sending them further north where we're wetter. So, as the climate changes, we help the trees migrate to places where they'll have a better chance of survival. It's a tiny grassroots kind of thing, and I don't know if any of our members will plant them, but it's worth a try."

Jo thinks of the sequoia groves to the south, all those ancient trees wrapped up in silver to protect them from fire. She can see their needles, leaking green from lack of water, turning drought brown and falling to cover the forest floor. She imagines Liam spiriting their cones away to safer ground.

"Will it work?" she asks.

Liam shrugs. "Who knows. It's being tried with a lot of different species. All over the world. It could be a disaster. We know too little about ecosystems and how they interact and the damage we can create with nonnative plants. But it's something. At least it's doing something."

Jo thinks of the little sequoia sapling growing in the pot on their back porch, tiny and fragile and still so very young. She remembers the way River gripped the cone in tiny toddler hands, the simple certainty in that demand to plant.

3

Jo sits at the rickety café table, the one that always has a coaster placed beneath one foot to try to stabilize it. She listens to the loud patter of ice and rain. Minutes before, she was ducking inside to escape the sudden hail.

Now, as she sips her large coffee, she isn't sure if the buzz that runs through her is caffeine or weather or the thrill of creation. She is piecing fragments of poems together, all those scraps of walnut-inked words scratched out by night or dawn or dusk, snatches of lines sung by roots and moss and mushrooms, whispers heard in the leaves of trees. The words grow into each other, reaching out, tangling up in their unfurlings. Once she has pieced them, she tries to glimpse them whole in broad daylight. Here, in all the human café bustle, she tries to make sure she still hears them. She thinks she still does. Most of the time, these days, they don't fade or disperse.

Jo watches the little pellets of ice pile outside the window. She is always astonished by the shifting faces of spring. The way the world moves so swiftly between the warmth of the sun and the recklessness of rain. Sometimes the day is overtaken by these flashes of hail, sudden shards of clouds in skyfall.

Jo drinks her coffee more quickly than she should. That morning, River woke before 4 a.m., eager for the day to begin.

River is perpetually impatient for daylight. Even now, perhaps especially now, they are like a leafcreature seeking the sun, bright as the glint off the water.

Today, Saturday afternoon, Liam has taken River to the zoo. Jo knows the route they will take, winding through the animals, the way they will stop longest at the bears—the black bears in their forested enclosure, the polar bears with their icy water tank. The bears are River's favorite. They will watch them with wide, wondering eyes. Jo loves to watch the wonder of River at the zoo, but she cannot stand the zoo itself, the containment of the animals, the way they are displayed like museum pieces. She cannot help but worry for them. Can they really be happy in such a human space, under the unrelenting gaze of so many human eyes?

The poem feels complete now, so Jo reads it, pen hovering, ready to adjust a misplaced line. Words move. The poem subtly shifts shape. When it has settled, she rereads and knows that it is right.

She pauses in the moment of its shape-finding, the sense of shared content. But alongside this, still, an unfinished quality. The poems live in her notebooks, in sheets of paper in the drawer of her desk. Most days, she prefers things this way, the privacy of it, the hiddenness of her creations. Liam has been nagging her to start sending her work out again, to try to publish more like she used to, before she started working so much, before they bought the house, before River was born. But she worries about trying to pull the poems apart, about containing them within printed pages, about pinning them under a glassy human gaze. There is something alive in them that she fears such containment could kill. Something wild in the poems, in her, in the way the words find their ways through her now. Sometimes she thinks they leaf her into some other kind of creature. Sometimes, she feels rooted in their agency, as if the poems are growing her. Perhaps, her poems are not meant to be shared.

Jo closes the notebook, puts away her pen, glances out the window. The hail has stopped. It has been replaced by a flurry of rain. There is a third of her coffee left, so she picks up a copy of the free alt weekly paper from the rack by the door and turns to the arts sections. She's been trying to go to more readings, trying to make little pockets of space for herself outside of her day job and motherhood. She is scanning the listing of literary events when an ad on the side of the page catches her eye.

The ad holds a picture, small in smudgy newsprint. But, even blurred, there is the pull of it. She recognizes Ness's work.

Midwave, the show is called. And there, in the listing, Ness's name and the dates. It opens that weekend.

Jo's breath is stuck somewhere in her chest. She can feel the sting of water prickling behind her eyes, the ache of it down in her throat.

She sees it again, the vision from the bus, the splash of the water, the fur and the skin. Ness is here in her city. Ness has not been in touch. She has not sent even a postcard.

4

That night, sitting down to dinner with her husband and child, Jo feels caught between worlds, tugged along by two diverging currents.

While River clutches pasta noodles in their bare hands, pulling them up to their mouth and dangling them over to bite, Jo tells Liam about the art show.

"I want to go," she says, "with River. With you too, if you want. I want them to meet."

Liam doesn't speak. He shakes his head and takes his dinner into the other room to eat with his laptop.

River frowns at her, their face covered in red sauce.

"Mom and Dad fight," they say, all serious disapproval.

As they go through the usual bedtime routine—Jo cleaning up the dinner dishes while Liam does pajamas, sitting all together on the couch for book time, waiting while River decides which stuffed animal to bring to bed that night—Liam avoids catching her gaze directly. She watches his shoulders turn rigid as he gathers himself away from her. It is only after River has gone to sleep that Liam begins to ask questions.

"How did you hear about the art show? Have you been in touch with her?" He looks at Jo with a probing suspicion that startles her.

"No. I saw an ad in the paper for it. I haven't spoken to her."

Liam seems relieved by this. She can see, in the relaxing of his expression, how much he thought, for a moment, she'd hidden.

"What if I don't want you to go? What if I'm uncomfortable with it?"

Jo chooses her words carefully, but not cautiously. "I think I have to, anyway."

"What if I don't want you to bring River?"

"I think I need to bring them too."

She knows she should have paused before that answer, that she should have put more hesitation in her voice. But she couldn't. She doesn't feel the hesitation that she should.

"What am I supposed to do with that? Does what I think about any of this even matter?"

She sees Liam's confusion, the way the fear of it is beginning to harden inside him, turning him unreachable.

"River isn't just ours. They're hers as well."

The certainty inside her grows stronger when she speaks it. And she realizes she has, over these years, rooted herself deep inside it. She will never be moved from the uncanny truth of it.

"I don't know how to believe that," Liam says.

"Then believe it as a metaphor for something real."

"This isn't just about you having an eccentric perspective or wanting to be with someone else or wanting some more exciting life. It's about our child."

"I know that," Jo insists. "Of course it's about our child. That's why it matters."

There is a long pause. They are speaking different realities. She knows their sentences go past each other, cannot seem to meet.

"And if I can't just go along with it?"

"Then leave me."

Her words take his away. Even she is surprised by their cruelty. She can see his sense of betrayal, his search for the right thing to say.

"What if I did?" Liam asks. He leaves the question hanging in the space between them.

She knows they both sense the edge they have come to, how close they are to tumbling off of it. They have come upon it so quickly, this gap that she thought they had closed years ago widening before them again. She thinks she should feel more afraid of it.

"I hope you don't," she tells him, trying to pull them back, but still rooted in her resolve. "I hope we can do this together."

5

That night she dreams the ghost forest, rising up from under waves. She sees the water move from ocean to estuary, down rivers and streams, branching outward.

She sees River's hand holding the sequoia cone.

Plant.

Plant.

River patting the dirt down around the potted tree. Roots breaking through the earthware, overgrowing the bounds of it, unfurling out and down into ground. Joining the rest of them. All the roots in their reaching, tangling up with each other.

The tree grows, tall and wide. So tall it looks onto the ocean, gazing over ghost forest, touching the befores and the afters in the sunfire and mistsmoke and rainflood, guarding the space made in landsea.

Underneath,
roots will tangle with ghosts.
                      Roots
to hold the living
to embrace the dead.
A cone to grow
   a devastating green.

6

Jo wakes into the familiar of the morning routine. She makes breakfast, simmering the oatmeal, buttering the toast, while River and Liam tend to the starts in the window. River touches the little leaves with a care beyond their years, while Liam names each plant. "Tomato, kale, cucumber. In a few weeks, they'll be ready to go out in the garden." Liam guides River's hands as they water the plants. They are both so gentle with all that new green.

"Beautiful," Jo says to the child and the husband and the plants and the morning itself. She hands Liam a mug of coffee, as if the magic of the vapor curling up from its surface, that space where liquid just begins to be air, could hold them together.

"Thanks," he says, but she cannot read his expression.

7

"Come with us," Jo asks Liam again the day before the art show, trying to reach across the rupture that has opened between them. She can see it in her mind, the four of them together. Ness meeting Liam. River there with all of them. All the most important people of their life, of her life.

Liam shakes his head. "I can't."

That night, Jo and Liam lie in bed, side by side, and do not sleep. She listens to Liam's breathing. She tries to discern what he is thinking. The space between them feels so tense she expects some of her husband's thoughts to leak out of him, into the air, float over and into her. She wonders if he feels it too, the edge they have come to, the way her mind is flailing, trying to find a way around, a bridge across. There is a way, she knows, for them to reach each other in this. There is always, there always has been, some way. A secret window. A trap door. A hidden path still overlooked. Always tenuous, always just solid enough. But, tonight, she cannot find it.

Later, when dreams have almost taken them, Jo reaches out her hand.

"Come with me," she says and pulls them from bed.

She takes them out into the night. Outside, in the circle

of the backyard, the moon is full and shining through the branches of the sequoia. The sky is packed with stars. She is astonished by the clearness, all those little points of light. Usually, in spring, the sky is all clouds, cozy and obscuring.

The grass is damp and cold on her bare feet. It glistens with silver. She pulls him close.

"You know," she says, "when we look at the stars, we're looking back in time. It takes so long for their light to reach us. The lifetimes of trees. Beyond. We can never exist in the same time. Humans and sky. There's always the gap."

It is as if he is looking into her. She can't see clearly in the dark, even with the fullness of the moon, but she can feel him drawing closer.

"It's so beautiful, the way you see. But so painful too."

She understands. She knows how deeply she has hurt him, how hard he has tried to understand it. She wonders if they can mend it, this space between them that is forever breaking, or if they will always be reaching across it.

The familiar of his hands on her arms, neck, breasts. The crisp clarity of sky that hovers over. The kiss she knew, from the first time they made it, was home.

They lie in the grass, unclothed in the chill, the spring of the air on their skin, tangling into each other. She is becoming leaves and soil, dew and dark, velveting over with moonlight, all bark and bone.

Liam holds her close, tight, like she will float away from him, as if the stars will claim her. It is the first time and the last time and all the times between. For a moment, she catches a glimpse of it, the whole constellation of them.

After, they lie together in the grass, watching the sky from their backyard.

"Are you going to leave me?" he asks her.

She is surprised by the question, by its directness. She cannot see his expression clearly in the dark.

"No," she says. "I don't want to leave you. I never have."

"Oh," he says, and she thinks she hears relief in his voice. And underneath the relief, something else, something darker, the unrelief of the forever trying.

"I'm surprised you haven't left me, though."

He shakes his head. "I'll never leave you."

"Why not?"

"I can't," he says. "You're in the roots of me."

8

The next day, on a sunny spring afternoon, Jo gets River ready to go, struggles with the child to put on pants and a shirt, chasing them across the house before they will submit to a coat. The shoes are a game. River balances using Jo's knee as she crouches. River angles their toes, puts their feet into the shoes, fastening the velcro across.

"Good job," Jo says.

They walk out the door holding hands. They hold hands as they walk down the street to the bus stop and as they wait for the bus. Jo is always nervous around roads, worried her child will escape her and run into danger.

"Stay close," she is always reminding. "Stop and look both ways."

She takes River on the bus whenever she can. She wants them to know public transit, to expect it, never to fear or be confused by route maps or transit passes or riding next to others.

Today, they take a seat in the front, look out the windows as the bus trundles its way toward downtown.

They are going to the art show.

That morning, she asked Liam, once more, if he wanted to come with them.

He shook his head, told her he needed to go to the gardening store. So, Jo and River will go alone. Ness will meet River

285

and Jo will know if what she knows about the child is true. She will be able to see it in Ness when she looks at them.

Now, beside her on the bus, River is restless, so Jo starts a story with them.

"This one," she says, "is about a selkie. Do you know what a selkie is?"

Jo holds River's hand as they disembark from the bus, weaving through the crowds of people on the downtown streets and ducking into the gallery two blocks away. The gallery is crowded too. The paintings peek at her through the gaps in the people: the crest of a wave, the gray of a horizon, a moment of undersea blue.

River stays close to her, unsettled, she can tell, by the crowd. Soon, they are reaching their hands up to her. Safe and high in her arms, they become entranced by all the people, the way bodies move through the room, pausing at paintings, stopping to talk.

Carrying the child, soothed by the familiar way River rests their hand on her shoulder for balance, Jo finds herself in front of a landscape she recognizes. A maple reaching out over the water. The bark is made of ripples. The water is dotted with the moonsun shadows cast by the leaves. In the sky, totality. Jo is caught in Ness's rendering of it, how it is so close to her own remembering, as if Ness has drawn out an image Jo has held in her mind for years. The cold strange of it. The impossible celestial meeting. The softedged hard-blurred apocalypse of sky.

"Jo?"

She hears the voice behind her, but it is hard to pull her eyes from the painting, for the way it holds her in the memory of a moment. River squirms in her arms, wanting to stand. She puts them down beside her, holds their hand again, turns to find Ness there.

"It's beautiful," Jo tells her.

Ness smiles. And Jo feels the familiar force, the way she is drawn to her, drawn into her, drawn into the strange magic in herself with her.

When Ness looks at the child, really looks at them, her eyes go wide. Jo can see the pause, the way her breath stops for a moment.

"Oh," Ness says when her breath finds its way again. It is more of a sound than a word, a sound made somewhere in the depths of her.

And Jo knows, then, that it is true. She feels a sense of completion, the fragments shifting into form, and she sees how she has been trying to find her way into this moment for years.

"Are they?" Ness is asking, beginning to hold the impossible.

Jo nods.

"Oh," Ness says again. A brighter sound this time. A sound of wonder.

"This is River," Jo tells her. "River, this is Ness."

The child reaches out their hand. Ness takes it and bends down to them, coming level at the eyes. Bluegray reflects bluegray.

"Are you selkie?" River asks.

Ness laughs, a deep light sound like the sudden flow of undammed water.

"Maybe something like that," she says.

River holds up their hands, spreads their fingers wide. "Have selkie hands."

Ness smiles, holds her own hands up. "Me too."

Jo can almost see the threads that twine between the two of them, strands of silver in the air.

"One day," Ness whispers to River. "I'll show you my selkie skin."

Jo starts in the undercurrent rising to surface. She is not sure how serious Ness's words are, how real or unreal. And, in that moment, she knows how River will drift away from her, not now, but one day, how they will inhabit places she cannot follow, how, perhaps, Ness will be the one who can.

But, at the art show, there is little time for words. Ness is pulled aways quickly.

"Wait for me?" she asks before going to answer questions about one of her paintings. "I'll only be a bit."

Jo nods. "We'll be here."

As Ness vanishes back into the crowd, River stares up at a painting that swirls in dark colors. At first, Jo thinks it is another depiction of waves but then River points and says "roots" and Jo looks more closely. There is something woody there. A spiral of vining. She realizes there is a bothness to the painting. Water and wood. Earth and ocean. It makes her think of the ways that bark can look liquid, the ways that a tree can seem to flow into the ground and out of it. It makes her think of the ghost forest. And the maple by the river, reaching toward the currents.

A series of paintings. They will stay with Jo long after she is no longer looking at them. Jo holds River's hand while she pieces together the story she thinks she is beginning to see in the images.

The first painting shows a wall, boarded up, holding a secret. Hands grip the fur to pull it out. Silvering velvet, the glow seems to shine from inside it.

In the second painting, a figure stands on the shore, pulling on the selkie skin. The moon is full and bright, but the figure is all shadow.

In the third painting, trees grow underwater, boughs like arms, woody fingers reaching. The selkie catches on them, leaving tufts of fur behind.

In the fourth painting, the selkie is human again, returned, holding the silver skin, walking back up the shore. Against the sky, the outlines of branches. The selkie's eyes reflect the moon, glint animal.

Jo stands a long time with the paintings, so long that River becomes restless, tugging at her for attention. Ness, Jo thinks, has made a new story. The selkie that returns. The selkie that moves between water and land, between human and not. The selkie that makes her home in that motion.

After the art show, once Ness has managed to slip away, they stop for pastries and coffee with plans to bring their snacks down to the river. While they wait for their order, Jo's phone buzzes with a text from Liam. *Still at the show? Might join if that's alright.*

Jo smiles, texts back where they will be, texts back for him to come.

"Liam's on his way," Jo tells Ness and watches her frown before nodding.

They bring their snacks to a bench on the esplanade, gaze out at the water.

"I wondered if you might come," Ness admits. She is watching River as they crumble a muffin, squeezing it in the palm of their hand, then letting the crumbs fall to the ground, dotting the mossy concrete like snow.

The marks of the surgery are long healed. Jo almost doesn't

think of it, now, the weeks of casts, the way the casts came off to show the angry skin, the wedges worn at night to keep the fingers apart, the massage three times a day for months to keep the scars from stiffening the joints. There were no complications. The fingers mended and grew. Now, River only holds the scars, small silvery vines leafing out from in between the fingers on each hand.

"You could have told me you were in town," Jo says to Ness.

Ness shakes her head. "I didn't want to bother you if you didn't want me to."

"I tried to find you," Jo says.

"I didn't really want to be found."

"I could tell."

They do not speak it, the pain of the leaving, the vanishing followed by vanishing, the ways they have both felt abandoned. Instead, they watch River for a while with the muffin. The child has moved on to picking out the berries, nibbling them from purpling fingertips. Jo scans the path for Liam, does not see him yet.

"So," Ness asks. "What have you been up to, in addition to this little riverling?"

Jo laughs. River is intent on their berries, ignoring the two adults and their grown-up talk.

"Writing mostly," she says. "I make my own ink now."

"Oh," Ness breathes. "You would. Will you teach me?"

Jo nods. "If you want."

"I'm in my sea witch phase. I've been thinking about making my own paints."

"Your new work is beautiful."

"It's different," Ness says. "Deeper somehow. Elemental feeling."

"Mine too."

They are silent for a moment. Jo thinks about the different feeling of Ness's new work. The way it has shifted again. The urgency in it now.

"I'm moving back," Ness says, "to the house on the coast. I've been fixing it up to live there."

Jo thinks of the house, her mind drifting all those years back to the paintings, the poems, the flood. She can hear the ocean. She can see the ghost forest lingering just under the water. And Ness's new paintings, the selkie skin hidden in the walls. Realities blur, dreams to waking.

"I'm trying to plant a garden," Ness is saying. "The backyard is so bare. Just grass. It needs trees and flowers and—"

"We have a tree," River interrupts. "Sequoia needs a home in the ground."

Ness laughs, uncertain.

"We do actually," Jo says. "River and Liam grew them from a seed."

"Wow," Ness says.

Jo sees her dream again, sees the way that they will *plant, plant.*

Here, now, by the river, they sit on the bench, three together. And then, up the path, she sees Liam walking, searching. She waves so he can find them.

Ness is watching River. There is a brightness that comes over her when she looks at them. River glances up from the crumbs, sees Ness looking, and gives her the glint of a smile. Then the child grabs Ness's hand and pulls her from the bench, moving down toward the water.

"I love wading," they say, leading Ness to the place where the gravelly banks meet the waves. Before Jo grasps what is happening, they are already splashing in ankle deep.

"Be careful," Jo calls after them.

Ness kicks off her sandals and splashes too, laughing a laugh Jo has never really heard from her before. There is a wildness inside it, a sound of ocean depths.

"I don't know if that water's safe for wading," Jo calls, thinking of pollution, all the sludgy things the currents collect as they wind their ways up the valley. She is disappointed in herself for thinking this, for letting the mother-worry bubble out of her.

Ness laughs again. A different kind of laugh. A laugh calibrated for the human ear.

"It's cleaner than it used to be. People swim in it now, you know? Safe enough."

Have you been swimming here? Jo wants to ask but doesn't. With your secret selkie skin?

Instead, she watches the wading, her feet rooted to the shore. Liam approaches slowly, trying not to intrude, uncertain of his place. She beckons him, watching the way River treads carefully over the gravel and rocks, sure to find the right foothold before shifting their weight. The way Ness moves with balanced confidence, gripping with bare toes, holding River's hand with assurance, as if she has always cared for the child.

Jo feels River's subtle shift as an echo in her own body. She can see it, almost, like a dream overlaid upon waking: Ness and River slipping into the water, a smooth quick dive, all fins and fur and silver. She blinks and the image disperses. It is simply the two of them holding hands and wading, the glow of the waves silvering their human feet.

9

Outside of time, she takes the child along the familiar path. Words rustle in her bag, tell her where they want to go. She has written them in walnut ink by night while her family sleeps. They have tendrilled like twigs and roots and branches, deep and golden, all these words she has found, this tiny ecosystem of poems she has made with them. Even now, they move inside her, around her, like spells.

Jo holds River's hand as they pass a group of cyclists weaving around the other walkers. She only has to pause once to orient herself, to remember the right direction. They find the deer trail easily. It's still in the same place it was, years before, branching off into the trees. She holds River's hand as they follow it. The trail is overgrown, at some points, with the twiggy reckless branches of saplings. They wind slowly into the spot she knows. They come to the vine maples, the fallen tree, the moss. Here, they sit, and eat the apples she has packed them all the way down to the cores.

The day is cloudy. A hint of mist lingers in the air. Jo thinks she can find it, here, now, with River, the path she and Ness walked on the day of the eclipse. She thinks it will open for them.

When they have finished the apples, they leave the cores near the fallen tree. "Ant food," River says as they poke around the undergrowth, observing the lichen and slugs. River hears the trickle of water first. They lead her to it, the channel that moves the tiny stream down to the river. It was dry in early fall, all those years ago when she and Ness found it. Now, the water moves through it, shallow as a finger's width, narrow as a hand.

She and River follow.

Down and around and into the heart of the place. She knows the way. She can feel the pull of it, same as the water can, a force as strong as a gravity.

They come to the maple, the big green leaves just beginning to unfurl into the season. River smiles up at her.

"A secret place," they say.

"You were made here," she tells them. "This place is inside you."

River thinks about this notion. She can almost see the movement of the thoughts, confusion shifting to resolve.

"Like apples," River tells her, holding their hands over their middle.

Jo nods. The poems are restless words inside the bag, bumping up against each other. And she knows, now, what they want, where they are trying to get to, who they have been made for.

"Let's dig," Jo says, pulling River down with her to the mud around the tree's roots.

They dig together with rocks and sticks. They dig with fingers and palms. They dig a hole, book-deep and paper-wide. The ground is damp. The mist curls around them. She can feel the pulse of the maple, moving to the sounds of the water.

Jo takes the poems from her bag and tucks them in the ground among the roots of the tree. She knows the draw of the underground, the way the words will seep into the soil as the paper dissolves, letting go of its form and merging back into the woods.

They push the mud over it, smearing it onto the pages, pat the dirt flat.

When they have done it, they sit, muddy and cold, beneath the maple, Jo perched on a large steady root and River nestling into her lap. They listen to the whispers of water. And Jo remembers how, once, this place was filled with moonsun shadows and the rush of a world's afterend.

She knows now, what she is and what she will be. She will be a poet of waterland, a writer of leafground, chronicling the cavernous pathways of roots, listening to the trees and recording their secrets of ecotones.

She will bury them all. Every word. Every poem. Sing them back into the ground that whispers them into her, completing the circle, the lifedeath of creation.

The poems will grow like seeds in the wild, flower into otherlings, drop into minds—human, crow, cat, maple, fern, mushroom—transformed by the ways of the underlands.

One day, she knows, she can see it as she moves her dirt and inkstained finger through her child's hair, River will find this place again. They will be older then and grown. Walking, they will stumble on the trail. Following, they will find another. They will know the ways of water over land. They will tread the path back to the place that made them. Salmon-like, they will hold the course inside.

They will come through the undergrowth, pushing through vines and branches. They will come to the maple with leaves so impossibly wide, all golden like slivers of sun, paperlight.

River will listen to the current and the wind. They will hear the hum of the ground underneath them. Then, the words will come. A poem. A story set in fragments. Their own. It will come to them

through sapblood and leafskin,
    wavebeat and raincry,
words to move through the whispers of the trees,
    tracing the ways of the water.

Acknowledgements

First, a huge thank you to Stillhouse Press for taking on my strange little book and to my editor, Kate Keeney, for all the care you have shown it. I am so grateful for your poetic sensibilities. Thanks to Taylor Schaefer for all your hard work to create publicity magic. Thank you Scott W. Berg for shepherding the book along. Thanks to cover designer Michael McDermott, artist Alex Giron, and interior designer Paul Logan for your beautiful work to give *Leafskin* such a resonate visual presence.

This novel was drafted while I was a PhD candidate in Bath Spa University's Creative Writing program and is a much better work than it otherwise would have been because of the thoughtfulness of my cohort and the attention, enthusiasm, and generous feedback of my advisors Tracy Brain, Gerard Woodward, and Jane Borodale.

Thank you also to the many institutions and teachers who have guided and supported my work along the way, including David Bosworth, Malinda Lo, Robin MacArthur, Chinelo Okparanta, Maya Sonenberg, Shawn Wong, the Bread Loaf Environmental Writers Program, the Tin House Summer Workshop, the Lambda Literary Writers Retreat for Emerging LGBTQ Voices, and the University of Washington Creative Writing MFA program.

A forest of gratitude to my dear writer friends who make up the ecosystem my work is able to grow in. Thank you to Justine Chan for your unwavering support and for that leaf necklace that settled me on this novel's title. Thank you to Audie Shushan for your belief in this book and the depth of your reading and insights. Thank you to Sabrina Mandanici for the immense gift of your eyes on these pages and the clarity you helped to bring out in the work. Thank you to Adriana Campoy, Alison Stagner, Rachel Linn, and Rachel Sanders for your conversation and inspiration over many years. And thank you Callum Angus for the generative generosity of your friendship and for all the walks and talks and wildflowers. Thanks to my partner Jason Kastrup for the strength of your love and the beauty of your whimsy and for working your microphone magic to produce the *Leafskin* audiobook.

Thank you to my family for your support and for all the times you watched my kid while I worked on this book. My dad, Christopher, for the gift of your curiosity, your steadfastness, and for always loving me whatever shape I take. My mom, Sandra, a writer who left us too soon, your love and creative spirit are a part of everything I am and make in this world. My brother, Zach, and his family, Nattasha and Helena, your steady glow is a constant inspiration. My mother-in-law, Mary Lynn, your care and artistry are a force of the warmest kind. My beloved cats, Mab and Luthien, thank you for your company through so many early writing mornings.

To the trees and ferns and mosses and flowers and crows and squirrels and racoons and ladybugs and bees and mountains and waterways and all the many beings of my Northwest home, my immense gratitude. Living among you, and trying to be in conversation with you, is the greatest privilege and the greatest responsibility.

My wife, Elanor Broker, your love and partnership have held our little world together through so much. I am so grateful for your witchy ways, the entwining of our writing, and to live my life alongside someone who loves the mysteries of moss in rain as much as I do. And Ash, our magical child, thank you for the brightness of your presence and the wonder of your imagination. So much of what I write, I write for you.

The Author

Miranda Schmidt (they/she) is a writer living in Portland, Oregon whose work circles around the folkloric, the familial, queer magic, and the more-than-human world. Their writing has appeared in *Triquarterly*, *Orion*, *Electric Literature*, *Catapult*, and more. She has received support from the Lambda Retreat for Emerging LGBTQ Writers and Bread Loaf Environmental Conference and taught creative writing at the Portland Book Festival, the Loft, the University of Washington, and Portland Community College. Miranda is a current PhD candidate at Bath Spa University and received their MFA from the University of Washington.

www.ingramcontent.com/pod-product-compliance
Lightning Source LLC
Chambersburg PA
CBHW061642190726
48289CB00006B/1701